TWELVE DAYS *and* TWELFTH NIGHT

BOOKS BY SARAH SUNDIN

When Twilight Breaks
Until Leaves Fall in Paris
The Sound of Light
Embers in the London Sky
Midnight on the Scottish Shore
Mists over the Channel Islands
Twelve Days and Twelfth Night: A World War II Christmas Novella

SUNRISE AT NORMANDY SERIES

The Sea Before Us
The Sky Above Us
The Land Beneath Us

WINGS OF GLORY SERIES

A Distant Melody
A Memory Between Us
Blue Skies Tomorrow

WINGS OF THE NIGHTINGALE SERIES

With Every Letter
On Distant Shores
In Perfect Time

WAVES OF FREEDOM SERIES

Through Waters Deep
Anchor in the Storm
When Tides Turn

a WORLD WAR II CHRISTMAS *novella*

TWELVE DAYS *and* TWELFT NIGHT

SARAH SUNDIN

Revell
a division of Baker Publishing Group
Grand Rapids, Michigan

Published by Revell
a division of Baker Publishing Group
Grand Rapids, Michigan
RevellBooks.com

Printed in the United States of America

Library of Congress Cataloging-in-Publication Data
Names: Sundin, Sarah author
Title: Twelve days and twelfth night : a World War II Christmas novella / Sarah Sundin.
Description: Grand Rapids : Revell, a division of Baker Publishing Group, 2026.
Identifiers: LCCN 2025050788 | ISBN 9780800747336 paperback | ISBN 9781493455638 ebook
Subjects: LCSH: United Service Organizations (U.S.)—Fiction | World War, 1939–1945—United States—Fiction | LCGFT: Romance fiction | Christian fiction | Novels | Fiction
Classification: LCC PS3619.U5626 T94 2026
LC record available at https://lccn.loc.gov/2025050788

This book is a work of fiction. Names, characters, places, and incidents are the product of the author's imagination or are used fictitiously. Any resemblance to actual events, locales, or persons, living or dead, is coincidental.

Cover photograph of couple dancing © Natasza Fiedotjew / Trevillion Images.

Cover design by Laura Klynstra

Published in association with Books & Such Literary Management, www.booksandsuch.com.

Baker Publishing Group publications use paper produced from sustainable forestry practices and postconsumer waste whenever possible.

26 27 28 29 30 31 32   7 6 5 4 3 2 1

In fond memory of Marcy Weydemuller,
a gifted writer and one of my closest friends.
I will miss her wise counsel, her honest challenges,
her deep insight, and her compassionate heart.

ONE

On the first day of Christmas my true love sent to me . . .
a partridge in a pear tree.

SAN DIEGO, CALIFORNIA
MONDAY, OCTOBER 18, 1943

Soft sunshine, a sea breeze, and a shining new opportunity. Maggie Oliver paused to savor the Italian Renaissance façade of San Diego's USO-Army-Navy YMCA building. Then she climbed granite steps and swung open the door.

A senior hostess sat at the front desk, her cherubic face crowned by silver hair.

"Good morning." Maggie mirrored her bright smile. "I'm Margaret Oliver, and I'm—"

"Late." All resemblance to a cherub disappeared in a great pinching of features.

A clock above the woman's head indicated Maggie was five minutes early, but she knew better than to argue. "I do apologize. The trolley—you understand."

The woman rose, barely taller standing than sitting. "Miss Perkins, please watch the front desk."

"Yes, Mrs. Laverne." A young brunette scampered over.

Mrs. Laverne marched across the red-tiled lobby under a wood-beamed ceiling. "I serve as one of the directors of this USO club. I'll show you to your office, Mrs. Oliver."

"Miss Oliver."

"Miss?" She cranked her gaze back to Maggie and almost stumbled. "When will USO-Camp Shows learn their lesson and stop placing responsibility in the hands of single young ladies? After the unfortunate situation with Miss Holmes . . ."

Unfortunate? Bernard Anderson, the Camp Shows regional director, had hired Maggie after Miss Holmes married.

Mrs. Laverne huffed and resumed her march.

Maggie trotted after the club director. Perhaps kind words would help. "Mr. Anderson told me about the important work you do at this club. He said you have over five hundred beds for servicemen on leave and offer lots of services and recreation."

"We do. We've had five million visitors since January. Do you see this tile floor? It was supposed to last ten years, but we had to replace it after only one year."

"Oh my."

Mrs. Laverne passed through an arched doorway and waved toward a gymnasium. "You can imagine what an imposition it is to sacrifice space for Camp Shows, but sacrifice we must."

Maggie lifted an eyebrow as she followed the woman up a staircase. Mrs. Laverne wasn't her supervisor, but she was opening precious space to a separate branch of the USO. "Thank you for making room for us."

On the second floor, Mrs. Laverne gestured to an open door. "Here's your office. Your assistant arrived fifteen minutes ago. Now, if you'll excuse me."

"Thank you." But Maggie's smile landed on the club director's retreating back.

Inside the office, a middle-aged woman strode up to Maggie, and her dark eyes pierced like an obsidian knife. "Come on. No time to waste. Let's get to work."

Well, that was an unusual way to be welcomed, but Maggie found a smile. "Good morning. I'm Miss Oliver—"

"San Diego's new Camp Shows director." The woman spread manila folders on the larger of the two desks. Gray streaked her neatly rolled black hair. "The Navy wants a Christmas show, but Miss Holmes waited too long. The Camp Shows troupes are already booked, so you'll have to start from scratch. Only two months till Christmas, and we've got nothing."

Maggie's head spun, so she removed her hat and straightened the jacket of her dark blue suit, the one Grandpa said made her eyes look as blue as Grandma's.

Sweet Grandpa. He was so proud of her, but this job was on a trial basis. If she couldn't pull a show together, she'd lose this job. And he'd lose his home.

"I've organized this for you." Miss Nameless slapped her hand on a folder. "Let's go."

So, Maggie had a hardworking assistant, and she joined her at the desk. "Your name is . . . ?"

"Ria Fernandez." She held out a folder, and a golden band sparkled on her ring finger.

Maggie set her hat and purse on the desk and took the folder. "Ria? That's pretty."

"Ria is short and fast." She flicked the folder. "The show, Miss Oliver."

Maggie settled into the wooden chair, and Mrs. Fernandez pulled over a chair beside the desk.

Putting on a show would be a thrilling challenge, and Maggie could do it. After over ten years dancing in Hollywood, she'd danced with USO-Camp Shows, then choreographed, then directed. This was the next step.

She opened the folder. "What do we have, Mrs. Fernandez?"

"Call me Ria. Save a lot of syllables."

"Is that so? Call me Maggie and save a few more."

Ria snapped up her gaze, and a smile burst out. "I like you."

Maggie laughed. "What do we have?"

"Nothing." Ria pointed to the folder in Maggie's hand. "List of venues, contacts, phone numbers. An *X* means they aren't available."

Maggie whistled. "That's most of them."

"You have appointments this afternoon at the three best options." Ria handed Maggie a neatly typed list. "Your schedule, your contacts, where to meet them, the trolley route."

"Oh my." Very efficient.

Ria slid over another folder. "Mr. Anderson gave me a list of Hollywood stars, but we'd better book them fast."

Halfway down the list, Maggie gasped. "Prescott Duke? He's my favorite star. I danced in three of his movies. Not with him, of course. Just in the ensemble. With his dark good looks, they always paired him with blondes, not brunettes like me. But, oh my. He's so handsome and such a gentleman, and that voice. It's like midnight blue velvet."

Ria cleared her throat, and the obsidian returned to her gaze.

Maggie gave her an apologetic smile. "Too many syllables?"

She tapped the list. "See the *X*? You don't want Mr. Duke. He was burned in an accident. Really bad scars."

"I—I'd heard." Prescott Duke's story had been the talk of the town. He'd been one of the first stars to enlist after Pearl Harbor, but his bus to the training camp had crashed and burst into flames. Mr. Duke had escaped but then returned to the inferno to save other men. He'd been discharged from the Army due to his injuries, and he hadn't made a film since.

The man was a hero, and Maggie slid her finger over the *X*. "I want him in my show. Scars and all."

Yeoman Third Class Frank Sebastian led Maggie toward the Old Globe Theatre in San Diego's Balboa Park. Modeled after the Globe Theatre in London from Shakespearean times, the circular building had half-timbering near the roof and Old English lettering.

With all her visits to the park, why had Maggie never been inside the theater? "I love it. I absolutely love it."

"We're mighty fond of it." The square collar of the sailor's navy-blue tunic fluttered in the wind. "It was built for the California Pacific International Exposition in '35. It was supposed to be torn down afterward, but the city rallied, raised money, and had it built to code."

The squawk of seagulls, the rustle of palm trees, and the scent of eucalyptus trees added a California layer to the charm. "Now the Navy runs it."

"Yes, ma'am. After Pearl Harbor, we took over most of the buildings in Balboa Park to expand the naval hospital. We use the theater for lectures and entertainment. We use the Museum of Man over yonder for a hospital ward."

Holding back her hair, Maggie turned in a circle. To the left of the theater, the Spanish-inspired museum raised an ornate stucco tower and a colorful tiled dome to the blue sky. "It's perfect."

"Don't get too excited, ma'am. The theater only seats about five hundred. You'd need multiple showings for all the sailors in San Diego, and the theater will rarely be available for rehearsals."

She followed the handsome blond sailor toward the theater. Frank Sebastian . . . the name was familiar, but the face wasn't. Since he was from the South and easily ten years her junior, she couldn't imagine where she might have met him.

He opened the door and led her through the lobby and into the theater.

Maggie strolled down the aisle. The stage was small, but she liked how the wall encircled the floor seating and how balconies stacked up that wall like bunk beds.

She could practically see actors in Elizabethan garb calling out lines. "Too bad Shakespeare wouldn't fit for a Christmas show. I can't see our boys sitting through a play in Ye Olde English anyway."

"That's what they thought for the Exposition too, so the Globe Players performed short versions of Shakespeare plays. They were a big hit. The scripts are in the office. Want to see?"

"Why, yes." Maggie followed the yeoman up the aisle. "Short versions?"

"Yes, ma'am. About an hour."

"An hour . . ." The men might sit through that, especially if it were a comedy, especially if supplemented by song-and-dance numbers and plenty of pretty girls.

Frank Sebastian entered an office off the lobby, shoved boxes aside, and opened a file cabinet. "Here we go. *The Taming of the Shrew*, *Hamlet*, *Twelfth Night*, *Macbeth*—"

"*Twelfth Night*? May I see?"

"Yes, ma'am."

Maggie took the thin script. "I played Olivia in this play in high school. I loved it. Full of comedy and mistaken identities. And . . . and Shakespeare wrote it for Christmas."

"Huh." The sailor screwed up one eye. "The fellows always like a good laugh."

Maggie clutched the script to her chest, and a plan danced in her head like a Busby Berkeley spectacular—the venue, the program. All she needed was a star.

LOS ANGELES, CALIFORNIA

Prescott Duke sat in a leather armchair in front of Melvin Underwood's shiny desk, and his foot jiggled. "Anything for me? Anything at all?"

Melvin rested his big hands on his big belly. "You know the answer, Press."

Prescott tugged at his shirt collar. "I know I'm done in movies. I know that. I mean, I'll do anything. A charity gig, a—"

"What are you worried about?" Melvin's thick gray eyebrows fused. "You have a fancy house, a fancy car, and enough money for life if you manage it well. And you do."

"It's not the money. It never was. I'd work for free."

"Never say that to your agent."

Prescott cracked a smile, then sobered. "I mean it, Mel. I'm going stir-crazy. It's been almost two years since the accident. I'm tired of doing nothing all day."

"What're you going to do? Get a job?"

Modern art hung on the paneled walls, a far cry from the tar-papered walls of the tenement where Prescott had grown up. "I've been thinking about it."

Melvin sighed and leveled his gaze at Prescott, hard but not unkind. "With those hands?"

He flinched and rubbed the gnarled skin. In the agonizing weeks in the hospital, he'd lost four of his fingers, two on each hand. Even holding a pen was difficult.

"Listen, kid. I'm not being mean, just realistic. You've got a sixth-grade education and no job skills. What're you going to do? Go back to the boxing ring where I discovered Joe Prescott and turned him into Prescott Duke?"

Heaviness filled his chest, and he shook his head. He had nothing but his voice. But with a mangled face, acting and singing were out of the picture.

Melvin fished a pear from the fruit bowl on his desk. "A lot of men would be happy to be retired."

"I'm only thirty-five. I shouldn't be retired."

"It's not too late to take up drinking." Melvin flashed a mischievous smile and bit into the pear.

Prescott was in no mood to play along. "Never."

"Wish I'd discovered you before you discovered God in that rescue mission. Would've made my job easier."

A tiny smile for old time's sake. If he'd played the bad boy role, he might have made the jump from B movies to the A list a lot earlier. But at what cost?

Melvin waved his pear in a little circle. "Find a hobby. Take up birdwatching or something."

"I've been reading a lot."

A quiet cuss, and Melvin's head drooped. "Whatever you do, promise you won't take up writing. Every actor thinks he can write. Every actor is wrong."

Melvin's secretary leaned in the door. "Mr. Underwood? Call for you from a Miss Margaret Oliver with the USO regarding a Christmas show for the Navy boys in San Diego."

"Put it through, Edna." He glanced at Prescott. "You don't mind?"

Prescott shook his head and waved his agent toward the phone.

Melvin set down the half-eaten pear, sandwiched the phone between shoulder and ear, and slid open a desk drawer. "Melvin Underwood here. How many dancing girls you need?"

Then Melvin's gaze shot to Prescott. "You want Prescott Duke?"

Prescott sat up straighter, his mouth hanging open.

Melvin held up his hand to stop him. "I'm sorry, Miss Oliver, but you must not have heard. Mr. Duke was badly burned in an accident. He—he has scars."

Prescott's face burned on the left side. Burned. But it was better for the woman to find out now than when he showed up for the first rehearsal.

Melvin ran his hand through his silver hair. "Yes. Yes, I understand stage is different from film . . . No, his voice wasn't affected . . . "

No, his voice wasn't affected, and Prescott edged forward in his chair.

"Sorry, lady," Melvin said. "You must have an old list, from before Pearl Harbor. He isn't available."

What? He'd been available for well over a year. Prescott sprang forward and snatched the phone right out of Melvin's hand. "Miss

Oliver? I am very much available. I would be honored to be in your show."

A feminine gasp. "Is that—Mr. Duke?"

Melvin groaned. "Press, you don't know what you're doing."

Prescott jabbed a finger at the phone. "The lady invited me to be in her show, and I want to do it. What else do I need to know?"

"Mr. Duke?" The woman's voice quivered. "I—I'm so sorry. I didn't know you were there. How much did you hear?"

"I heard that I have a chance to do something worthwhile with my sorry life for the first time in almost two years. What would you like me to do?"

"Oh. Well. Serve as the emcee and sing a song or two, dance perhaps. I hadn't thought that far. And we're doing a short version of Shakespeare's *Twelfth Night*. I thought—with your name—I thought maybe you could play the role of Duke Orsino."

"Anything. I'll be a stagehand, water boy, whatever you want. I'm yours, Miss Oliver."

"Oh." She gave a nervous little laugh. "Thank you."

Melvin rolled his eyes.

Prescott hadn't meant to sound flirtatious, and he raised a sheepish smile.

"Fine." Melvin grabbed his gold pen and took back the phone. "All right, Miss USO. Where does he need to be and when?"

Prescott settled back into the armchair.

This wouldn't solve his problem, not by a long shot. But for two months, he could fill the void of his life.

SAN DIEGO
THURSDAY, OCTOBER 21, 1943

Prescott stepped off the trolley at the streetcar terminal on Park Boulevard. He tipped his hat lower over his brow. Miss Oliver hadn't seen his scars yet. Perhaps she'd change her mind.

A brunette approached with a USO armband around the sleeve of her wine-colored suit, and her smile grew with each step. "Mr. Duke, thank you for coming. I'm Maggie Oliver."

"Thank you for inviting me to be in your show."

Pretty blue eyes studied him, and her smile deepened and softened, as if searching behind the scars without ignoring them.

Something about her touched memories. "Pardon me, but have we met?"

"Not formally, but I danced in *Hollywood Harmonies of 1938*, *Hollywood Harmonies of 1939*, and *Hollywood Harmonies of 1940*."

Prescott chuckled. "And you still asked me to be in your show."

"That's *why* I asked you. Oh, here's Petty Officer Sebastian." She waved to a tall blond sailor in dress blues. "He's our ticket to get in. And this." She handed Prescott a USO armband.

"Thank you, Miss—"

"Please call me Maggie. As my assistant says, 'Save a lot of syllables.'"

"Then call me Prescott." With the clumsy remainder of his hand, he wrestled the armband over the sleeve of his suit.

After Maggie introduced him to Petty Officer Sebastian, the yeoman showed a pass to the guards and led them through the gate.

"Welcome to Balboa Park." Maggie pointed to a stately white building. "That's the Natural History Museum."

"Now it's a ward for the naval hospital," the sailor said in a Southern accent. "Nine hundred sixty beds."

Dozens of men in light blue robes milled about the plaza, walking in pairs, rolling in wheelchairs, lounging on a strip of grass.

Over six months Prescott had spent in an Army hospital. "Will the patients attend our show?"

"Only the convalescent ones, sir." Sebastian led them along an arcaded walkway with ornate Spanish-style carvings. "That building across the way holds another five hundred patients. Three thousand beds in the main naval hospital and another three thousand in this here Balboa Park annex."

Six thousand patients. Prescott frowned, pulling at the scar tissue on his left cheek. "Those who are confined to bed—can we do something for them?"

"Please, sir." Sebastian turned a bright smile to him. "Visiting stars often tour the wards."

"I'm here for two months. If I can help in any way . . ."

"Yes, sir. I'll see to it."

The shade of the arcade ended, and they entered a sunshine-filled plaza.

Maggie smiled at a rectangular pool and a long, airy building constructed of arched wooden beams. "The Lily Pond and the Botanical Building. My favorite part of the park. I always thought the Lily Pond would be a dramatic setting for a good cry."

Only show people would look at the pond in such a way, and Prescott smiled.

"The Lily Pond is now used for rehabilitation." Sebastian gestured toward the dozen men swimming in the waters.

"Are you from San Diego?" Prescott asked Maggie.

"Iowa, actually. But my mother is a San Diego girl, and we took the train to California every few years to visit my grandparents. And I visited often after I came to Hollywood." Joy radiated from her voice. "Come along. I can't wait to show you the Old Globe Theatre."

"You mentioned a Shakespeare play." An unusual choice for a USO show.

"*Twelfth Night*, but a short version, only an hour, plus variety show numbers—two hours total. A fun Christmas show for the boys."

"Won't feel like Christmas for most of them." Prescott waved to the palm trees bobbing their shaggy green heads above the Spanish buildings.

Maggie laughed and tipped up her chin to the tropical greenery. "And a partridge in a palm tree," she sang in a full-throated soprano.

Prescott laughed in return, and the song tinkled in his head. "'The Twelve Days of Christmas.'" His feet stopped as the song and an idea revolved around each other like ballroom dancers. "*Twelfth Night*."

Maggie spun to him, and her eyes widened to the idea. "What if . . . ?"

"How many variety show numbers do you need?"

"Three to five minutes each . . . one hour . . ." She gasped. "Twelve."

"What if . . . ?"

"Each number inspired by one of the days of Christmas."

"Nine ladies dancing."

"Ten lords a-leaping." Maggie's laugh broke free. "I can see it.

As Duke Orsino says in *Twelfth Night*, 'If music be the food of love, play on.'"

It was brilliant. And Prescott hadn't had such an enjoyable conversation in almost two years.

"Miss Oliver? Mr. Duke?" Sebastian beckoned.

They'd fallen behind. Prescott and Maggie grinned at each other and rushed to catch up.

"It's perfect." Maggie splayed one hand like a sunburst. "I asked your agent for nine more men to complete the cast of *Twelfth Night*. There are three female parts in the play, but I asked for nine ladies, plus a starlet. He's sending Lola Lockhart—you starred with her in one of the *Hollywood Harmonies*."

"Yes, *1939*." He'd hoped never to see Lola again, but he kept his expression neutral. If she was volunteering for USO shows, perhaps she'd changed her selfish ways.

In a few minutes, Frank ushered them into the circular Globe Theatre.

Maggie stopped at the top of the center aisle. "Don't you love performing in a theater?"

"I never did." Prescott rested his hands on a wooden seat back. "Straight to the movies."

"Is it true what the movie magazines said? Raised on the tough streets of Chicago, discovered in a boxing ring?"

He gave her a look equal parts scoffing and teasing. "You don't read those rags, do you?"

"I do. I take them with a grain of salt, but salt is rather tasty."

Footsteps thumped into the back of the theater, and a sailor waved at Sebastian. "Frank? Lieutenant Jeffers needs to see you on the double."

Sebastian winced. "He knows I'm with the USO people."

"He says it won't take long."

"Stay here." Sebastian held up one hand to Prescott and Maggie. "I'll be back."

"Yes, sir." Maggie raised a playful salute. "We'll wait for our chaperone."

After Sebastian followed his colleague outside, Maggie sauntered down the aisle toward the stage. "So, the magazines—truth or Hollywood hokum?"

Prescott sauntered after her. "Both. Mean streets of Chicago and boxing ring—true. But they glossed over anything that clashed with the studio's image. Nothing sophisticated about a school dropout at twelve or a hoodlum at fourteen or a hobo in a rescue mission at twenty-two."

At the base of the stage, Maggie turned to him, eyebrows high and drawn together. "How awful. I never would have guessed."

"When Melvin discovered me, he sent me for lessons in diction and etiquette, as well as singing and dancing." Prescott owed Melvin everything.

Maggie's red lips rolled in, and concern grew in her gaze. "Shakespeare—will you be able? I could help."

"I should be fine. I was a good student, loved reading. Still do."

"Why did you drop out?"

The pain of the years after his father's death and his mother's remarriage threatened to swamp him, but he wrestled up a wry smile. "Education is a luxury I couldn't afford."

Maggie huffed. "I'm sorry. You'd think I'd know better after the Depression. I'm so spoiled. My father's a lawyer."

"Never apologize for the blessings in your life."

A grateful smile dimpled her cheek. "I have so many blessings.

For one thing, my big brother also became a lawyer, freeing me to disappoint the family by going to Hollywood." Humor glinted in her eyes.

Prescott couldn't imagine her disappointing anyone. "Why did you leave Hollywood?"

"Oh, I dance well, sing well, act well—but not well enough to break out. The only reason I could afford food was because I typed scripts for the studio. Then when I turned thirty, I realized I was never getting my big break. So I joined the USO. One story ended, and a new one began."

Prescott sank into a seat in the front row. His story had ended, but he saw nothing ahead. Nothing.

"What's the matter?" Maggie asked.

The silence of the theater. The emptiness of the stage. "You moved on after Hollywood. I wish I could."

"Of course you can." Confidence shone in her lovely face.

"Do you always see the bright side?"

She shrugged. "If I can't, I make a bright side."

How was that even possible? And why did he feel comfortable confiding in this woman, practically a stranger? "Since the accident, my life has been a blank page. Nothing but endless blank pages ahead of me."

"Then write on them."

"Write on them?"

"Yes." Maggie dashed up the steps onto the stage, then posed with her arms spread wide. "Write a new script for your life."

A new script? So many blank pages, riffling before him. Could he write on them? What would it look like?

"Not now, Prescott." With a mock stern look, Maggie wagged a finger at him. "For the next two months, you're under the heels of a cruel USO director." She performed a cramp roll—toe, toe, heel, heel.

Prescott rose from his seat, and with his gaze planted on that USO director, mimicked the tap-dancing step.

Perhaps over the next two months, he could mimic her bright-side-making, new-script-writing ways.

TWO

On the second day of Christmas my true love sent to me . . .
two turtle doves.

MONDAY, OCTOBER 25, 1943

The Little Theater in the USO club was designed for lectures or small ensembles, but it would meet Maggie's needs for today's cast meeting and auditions.

"I hope it meets your expectations." Acid dripped from Mrs. Laverne's words.

Poor Mrs. Laverne. Since the Old Globe was rarely available for rehearsals, on Friday Maggie had begged her for the use of the gymnasium—in the presence of Mr. Hutton of the local USO Advisory Board. Charmed by Maggie, Mr. Hutton had insisted that Mrs. Laverne accommodate her, including the Little Theater if the gym was occupied.

Maggie gave the older woman an acid-neutralizing smile. "It's perfect. I know it's inconvenient for you. If you'd like, the ladies in the cast could volunteer in the club."

"I think not." Mrs. Laverne lifted her cute little round nose.

"Our junior hostesses come from good families, girls with sterling reputations, not the Hollywood sort."

Camp Shows also had high standards, but Maggie kept her smile in place. "Very well."

After the club director left, Maggie placed her portfolio and clipboard on the podium.

"Maggie?" Violet Lane entered, as beautiful and willowy as when she and Maggie had danced together in the movies.

Maggie hugged the blonde, a few inches taller than she, and she studied her young face. "It's so good to see you, Vi. I was thrilled to see your name on the list. How long have you been with the USO?"

"Over a year. So far, they've sent me to Australia and Alaska. San Diego seems tame." Her green eyes sparkled.

Maggie peeked out into the hallway, then ushered Vi to the front row. "You'll never guess who's in our cast. Prescott Duke."

"You had a crush on him, didn't you?"

"Sh!" Maggie's finger flew to her lips.

"Wasn't he burned? Scarred?" Vi whispered. "Such a shame. He was so handsome."

"He still is," Maggie murmured. "His eyes, his voice. Who wouldn't have a crush?"

Vi shrugged and fingered a gold pendant around her neck.

A dove. She still wore it.

Vi's fiancé had been lost at sea not long after Pearl Harbor, and Vi had been mourning when Maggie met her in January 1942. Vi said her fiancé had given her the pendant because they were turtle doves, together forever.

Laughter and footsteps arose in the hallway. Maggie grabbed her clipboard and checked in the cast members at the door.

Two polished black shoes stopped before her. "Prescott Duke."

She looked up and laughed. He was indeed handsome, even with mottled pink scars on the left side of his face, contracting his smile and one eyelid. Worse than the scars was the sad wistfulness about him, so she gave him her brightest smile. "Please have a seat, Prescott."

After she checked off all the names—except Lola—she went onstage and welcomed everyone. "While we're waiting for Lola Lockhart, I'd like to introduce our star, Prescott Duke." She waved to him in the back row.

Prescott's eyes rounded, his mouth twitched, but he rose to standing.

Stares, attempts not to stare, attempts to meet his gaze, and Maggie's chest caved in. Surely, he had to deal with that every day.

"You may recognize my name," he said in that blue velvet voice, and he touched his scarred cheek with a dry smile. "But you may not recognize my face. I wear this mask so no one will be blinded by my stunning good looks."

Cast members chuckled, tight at first, then relaxing, and Maggie's chest filled in again.

"I'm honored to be here. Miss Oliver has an excellent show planned." He gestured to her and took his seat, very un-starlike.

Maggie checked her watch. Lola was fifteen minutes late, but Maggie needed to begin. She laid out the plan for *Twelfth Night*, with Prescott as Duke Orsino and Lola as Viola, and for twelve variety acts.

She held up her portfolio. "Prescott and I had some ideas for the twelve acts, but I'd like to see what you can come up with based on your individual skills—songs, dance, comedy, magic acts, acrobatics, ventriloquism . . ."

Ria bustled through the door with an armload of scripts. "Just typed up the last one."

"Thank you." The USO had removed the naughty bits from *Twelfth Night* to meet the organization's wholesome standards, and Maggie and Ria had spent the weekend typing.

"Mr. Underwood called." Ria handed Maggie a slip of paper.

Maggie read it and groaned. Lola Lockhart had dropped out after receiving a better offer, and the two actresses Mr. Underwood recommended were comedians, not leading ladies. "No one else?"

"All booked."

Maggie needed a Viola, a songbird to sing with Prescott. She scanned the room—nine beautiful and talented young ladies.

She hefted up a smile. "We have one more role to audition—Prescott Duke's leading lady."

Lola couldn't come? A sigh of relief, but then Prescott frowned. Since his own star no longer shone brightly, the show needed a woman with presence.

Such a loss would kill a movie, but Maggie shuffled papers with her confident expression intact. "Ladies, I'll have you each read a scene with Prescott and sing with him. How about 'White Christmas'? Everyone knows it. The scene starts on page twelve."

Wearing a light gray suit, Maggie passed out scripts. "Gentlemen, you'll audition for parts after the ladies. Read the cover sheet and decide which roles suit you. For each role, find the page number for the audition scene. Practice quietly in the back of the room."

Chairs scraped, and Prescott held out his hand for his script.

Instead of filling his hand, Maggie gestured to the front row. "Come find your Viola."

"Shouldn't I read too?"

She cocked her head. "You're Duke Orsino."

"The other men should have a chance."

A soft chuckle floated from Maggie's mouth. "Remarkable."

"Pardon?"

"You're the star. Every sailor in San Diego knows your name. They're coming to see you in the leading role." She waved toward the front row. "Come. Are you familiar with *Twelfth Night*?"

"I read it over the weekend." He followed her and sat up front.

"Great fun, isn't it? The mistaken identities, the plot to humiliate Malvolio, Viola dressing as a man and fooling everyone. The sailors will love it."

If only Prescott had noticed Maggie on the movie set. Her optimistic decisiveness, blended with kind inclusiveness, appealed far more than shining hair and eyes and smile—which she also had in abundance.

Maggie handed him a script at last. "You'll make a great Duke Orsino."

"Only man left in Hollywood, huh?" He cracked half a smile.

Her mouth puckered on one side. "There were a dozen men on the list. I wanted you. Talent is common in Hollywood, but gentlemen are rare. Besides, you smiled at me once."

Prescott cringed. "Once? That doesn't say much for how I treated the dancers."

"Oh, you were wonderful. No, this was special." Dark eyelashes dipped, and her gaze swung to the stage. "The director was jumping down the throat of the new girl, had her in tears.

I was coaching her, but the other girls laughed at her. So, I gave them a talking to."

"I remember that." He could picture Maggie with one hand on her hip, the other on the shoulder of the young dancer, reminding the girls that they'd all been new once and that the routine would fail unless they worked together.

She'd stood up for the vulnerable.

"That smile told me you care how others are treated." Maggie shifted papers in her lap. "First up, Violet Lane. Vi, are you ready?"

"I am." A lady floated up to the stage with the blonde good looks of Betty Grable, but with a soft glow that reminded him of Greer Garson.

"She has the right name," Prescott murmured to Maggie, then he found the scene and joined the blonde on the stage. He'd have to read cold, not easy with the difficult language.

But Violet Lane made it easy. She read with lively intelligence, easy emotion, and elegant gestures. Most importantly, she didn't simply perform for the audience, she engaged with Prescott.

"Thank you," Maggie said after only one page. "'White Christmas.'" She hummed a note to establish the key.

From the first line, their voices harmonized and blended as if designed for each other, and Maggie's jaw hung slack.

After the first verse, she beckoned Prescott to her. "What do you think?" she whispered.

"She acts. She sings."

"She dances too."

"Better than all that, she has presence. She's my Viola." He stared up at the pretty blonde. Why wasn't she already a star?

The setting sun cast golden light on Grandpa's darling bungalow, Maggie's home since she'd moved to San Diego after joining the USO.

At the same time, Grandpa had come home from a long stay in the hospital after breaking half a dozen bones falling off the roof.

Maggie crossed the lawn edged by Grandma's flowers, dormant for the autumn. After Grandma entered the sanitarium for tuberculosis, the ladies from Grandpa's church kept the garden going, knowing what it meant to him. Knowing the man could kill flowers with a single touch.

A sparrow hopped across the path. Grandpa and Grandma had been turtle doves too, meant for each other.

Would Violet Lane ever find another love? If the way Prescott had looked at her meant anything, it could be soon.

A twinge of pain in Maggie's chest, and she puffed it away. Crush or no crush, both Prescott and Vi deserved happiness.

Maggie opened the front door and crouched down. "Hello, Tobias."

Tobias bounded over, one ear pricked, the other floppy, and Maggie ruffled the mutt's gray and white fur. Grandpa had found the puppy on the streets the day Grandma died, and Tobias had absorbed all the love Grandpa poured upon him and poured it right back.

"I'm home, Grandpa." She hung her purse and hat by the door. "Let's have a quick dinner. *Thank Your Lucky Stars* is playing at the North Park Theatre, and you're my date."

In the living room, Grandpa sat in his armchair with his canes beside him.

With a stony expression.

How unlike him. "Grandpa?"

"I got a letter from your father today. You wrote to him, told him about my money troubles. Without asking me."

Maggie tensed, gave him a sheepish smile, and passed him to enter the kitchen. "I knew you wouldn't like it, but I also know Papa has plenty of money."

"Why does he have plenty of money? Because he doesn't spend it."

True. Maggie grimaced and pulled a can of tomato soup from the cupboard.

"Why would you do such a thing?" Grandpa frowned over his shoulder, over the countertop.

Maggie squeezed the can opener over the lid. "I wrote that letter right before I got this job. I didn't think they'd give it to me, and you told me—"

"That was for your ears only."

And only under duress after she'd seen his bank book. Maggie cranked the key of the can opener. Grandpa had sold his hardware store to pay for Grandma's treatments. His own hospital bills had depleted his savings. Even with Maggie's wages, they couldn't cover expenses.

Maggie dumped the soup into a pan with a satisfying slorp. "I thought Papa could help."

"He already does."

"He does?"

"We were doing fine." A growl lowered his voice.

Maggie hadn't heard that growl since she and her little sister,

Rose, had dug up Grandma's gazania. She opened the icebox and removed a bottle of milk.

Grandpa huffed. "Because you meddled—"

"Meddled?"

"Meddled. Now your parents are coming out for Christmas. Even though civilians aren't supposed to travel. Your father is going to sell the house and make me live with them in Iowa."

Maggie measured one can of milk and poured it into the pan. "Papa can be exasperating, but he can hardly force you out of your own house."

"It's no longer my house. He owns it."

Maggie spun to face him, dribbling milk over the stove. "How is that . . . ?"

Grandpa tapped one cane on the floor. "I was in the hospital a long time, had a couple surgeries. Your father offered to pay my medical bills, but I didn't want a handout. So I sold him the house. He lets me live here rent-free."

Which meant Papa didn't need Grandpa's permission to sell. "Oh no."

"With your wages and the money left after I paid the doctors, we've been fine. Your dad even sends a bit each month. We're fine."

Then Maggie had to open her big mouth. Papa must have spent a substantial chunk of his savings to bail out Grandpa, and now Maggie had asked him for more money? Papa was well-off, not wealthy, and his charity had limits.

"I don't want to live in Iowa." Grandpa's voice roughened. "I've lived in San Diego all my grown-up days. Met your grandma here. Raised your mama here. I had this house built."

Maggie's vision blurred, and she wiped milk driblets off the stove, where Grandma had cooked countless meals for the man she adored.

"I—I couldn't take Tobias." Grandpa buried his hand in the fur of the dog at his side.

"Rose." Maggie's sister was horribly allergic to dogs, and she would live with Papa and Mama forever.

Guilt flickered in Maggie's chest, but she hauled in a deep breath and lit the stove. "Never fear. I'll write to Papa and—"

"You'll do no such thing."

"But my new job pays more. I already told him I received the job—although on a trial basis. I just need to—"

"No, I'll write. I'll tell him it was a misunderstanding and not as dire as you thought."

"I could—"

"No." Grandpa aimed a finger at her. "The best thing you can do is keep your pretty little nose out of it."

"Oh, Grandpa." Maggie stirred the soup and blinked away the moisture in her eyes. "I'm sorry I disappointed you."

A deep sigh emanated from Grandpa's chair. "Oh, Maggie-mine, you could never disappoint me. Never. You have your papa's gumption—and sometimes it gets the better of you. But you also have your sweet mama's compassion."

"I just want to help."

"You want to help? Pray."

Maggie balanced the spoon in the pan and darted out to her Bible and notebook by her favorite armchair. "I'll add it to my list. I'll pray that Papa will understand, that he won't sell the house, that my show goes well so I'll get this job permanently, that—"

"That's a lot on your list."

Maggie jotted down every detail. "I do keep the Lord busy."

"Oh, Maggie-mine. Don't forget. Prayer is more than listing. It's listening."

She didn't quite know what he meant, but she smiled at him.

"I'll tell you how you can start." Grandpa tried to look stern again, but how could he when he had the sweetest brown eyes in the world? "Start by listening when the Lord tells you not to meddle."

"I don't meddle. I help."

He arched one white eyebrow. "If you're keeping secrets, you're meddling."

Maggie stood, planted a kiss on his forehead, and returned to the kitchen. "The only secret I'm keeping is how much cheese I'll put in your sandwich, and I'm not telling."

"Meddling." But Grandpa chuckled, and all was well again.

For the first time in his week in San Diego, Prescott had not ordered room service.

Since his accident, he went out in public as little as possible. Business meetings, doctor appointments, church. That was it.

Tonight he'd eaten in the hotel dining room, and he was strolling down Broadway toward the bay in the blacked-out evening, lit only by partial headlights on trolleys and cars.

The passersby paid him no mind, civilians intent on getting home or sailors searching for a bar or dance hall.

For the most part, the restaurant patrons had also paid him no mind. Those who had looked his way looked too long. After his first big movie hits, he'd attracted those looks, followed by a flash of recognition and "Is that Prescott Duke?"

Now those long looks were followed by revulsion or pity.

For almost two years, that had kept him inside. But today, the cast had overcome their initial shock and accepted him.

Prescott passed a newsstand, each page of each newspaper filled with words. "Write a new script for your life," he murmured.

His current script stank. He might have money and a nice house, but he had no people, no purpose. His idleness grated—it wasn't right, and it wasn't good for him.

He waited for a taxi to pass, and he crossed the street, dodging a trio of chatting office girls.

The last time his life had been empty, Melvin had rescued him. But this time, Melvin couldn't rescue him.

To his right rose the grand USO-Army-Navy YMCA. A crowd of sailors trotted up the steps, under the engraved sign reading "Young Men's Christian Association."

How many nights had Prescott spent at the Y in his youth? The Y had saved him.

Prescott chuckled. Neither Melvin nor the Y had saved him. God had. And that rescue could never be taken away.

His pace picked up, harder, faster. God didn't want him to sit around idle. He'd sent Prescott to this place at this time for some reason.

"What is it, Lord?" He wanted to do something good with his life. He wanted to help people. But how?

In a few blocks, he got as close to the bay as the Navy allowed. Piers jutted out, bristling with gray warships. In the harbor, silver starlight winked on the black waters, and on the far side, North Island stretched in a dark band.

If Prescott's life were a Hollywood script, it would be rags to riches . . . to rubble. Who would watch a movie like that?

For a movie to lift people up, it would need to be riches to rubble . . . to rebirth. To rebuilding. To refreshing.

Prescott would watch a movie like that.

A man, the hero, has everything. Loses everything that matters to him. Even as he retains what most people want. Yet he rebuilds his life, a better life, a life focused on others, not self. On community, not commodities.

Prescott's gaze lifted to the star-littered sky. He could see the man. Prescott could play him, but he wasn't Prescott. Not at all.

"Who are you?" he asked the man. "What did you have? What did you lose? What will you do now?"

He could envision a scene, like a movie in his head, hear the voices.

The man is wealthy, has it all, beautiful family he loves but neglects—due to the work he loves even more. He loses his family. His fault somehow. Loses his work.

More scenes. Dialogue. Side characters.

Although Prescott stood still, his breath came fast.

It was a story. What was he supposed to do with it? He was finished in film—he couldn't play the hero.

Could he write it? A screenplay?

Prescott groaned and stuffed his pitiful hands in his trouser pockets. How could he write? He had no schooling. And his hands—he couldn't write more than two sentences without pain.

No, he couldn't write a screenplay.

Yet fresh cool sea air filled him. A sense of hope. If he could imagine a new life for this imaginary man, perhaps he could imagine one for himself.

THREE

On the third day of Christmas my true love sent to me . . .
three French hens.

WEDNESDAY, NOVEMBER 3, 1943

In the gymnasium, three trios of ladies rotated in three circles, fingertips touching high in the center of each circle.

"That's lovely." Maggie noted the choreography on her clipboard. "Glide for three more bars, skirts held to the side, then break into a line and pirouette."

For the "nine ladies dancing" number, the nine women would dance to "Silent Night" in long silvery gowns bedecked with sequins.

On the far side of the gym, laughter flowed as the ten men practiced the "ten lords a-leaping" number. The men would sing "God Rest Ye Merry, Gentlemen" while breaking into solo leaps—balletic, acrobatic, athletic, comedic.

Prescott performed a *tour jeté* punctuated by uppercut punches. Elegant yet manly. As the magazines had proclaimed him, "Noble as a duke, but tough enough to put up his dukes."

Two of the men clapped Prescott on the back. He laughed, all shyness gone, and Maggie's heart warmed.

"Miss Oliver?" Ria entered the room with a stiff smile.

On her heels came Bernard Anderson, the Camp Shows regional director and Maggie's boss.

Maggie wore a short dance skirt and a cotton blouse knotted at the waist. She silenced a groan and put on a sheepish smile. "Welcome, Mr. Anderson. I apologize for my attire. We're choreographing."

"As is expected." Mr. Anderson's long face crinkled as a smile bent his gray mustache. "I had a meeting in town with a donor and thought I'd check in, seeing as how we gave you a difficult assignment with short notice."

"It's coming along marvelously." Maggie led Mr. Anderson and Ria to the rolling chalkboard at the side of the room. "Ladies, keep working on the choreography. Prescott, would you come here, please? Mr. Anderson, I'd like you to meet Prescott Duke."

"An honor." Mr. Anderson shook Prescott's hand. "I'm a big fan."

"Thank you, sir."

"Excuse me, Mr. Anderson." Mrs. Laverne marched into the gym. "I was told you were here. I'd like to lodge a complaint about the inappropriate use of the YMCA."

Maggie's cheeks burned. Inappropriate? How could she say such a thing?

Across the gym, the women tried a step, failed, and broke into laughter.

Mrs. Laverne waved toward the girls. "My club has been invaded by these—these cackling hens. And their indecent costumes and loose morals."

Maggie gasped. "Loose—"

Ria clamped a hand on Maggie's arm.

"Loose morals?" Mr. Anderson said with a concerned frown. "Have there been any incidents?"

"None, sir," Maggie said in a taut voice. "And we wear street clothes when we arrive and leave."

Mr. Anderson leveled a gaze at Mrs. Laverne that said he was open to complaints—but only reasonable ones. "Any incidents?"

"Well, no, but I don't see why our boys need this Hollywood hoo-ha. It would be seemlier to have the cast sing Christmas carols."

"Your concerns are noted." Mr. Anderson gave her a firm look. "Remember, the Advisory Board approved this use of the club. If any incidents do arise, please inform me. Good day."

"Good day." Mrs. Laverne averted her gaze and left the gymnasium.

Mr. Anderson turned that same firm look to Maggie. "I know the cast will follow the standards in the Camp Shows contract. Now—what do you have?"

Maggie smiled away her annoyance and showed off her chalkboard. After she introduced the grand outline of the show, she pointed to the first square. "First number, a solo with our leading lady, Violet Lane, in a swing on a pear tree in a gown flowing with white feathers, singing 'White Christmas.' Second, a tap dance number to 'Winter Wonderland,' with the whole cast in pairs, the men in top hats and tails, the ladies in red coats. Then the first of five acts of *Twelfth Night*. Mrs. Fernandez is working with the San Diego Community Theater to borrow Shakespearean costumes."

Mr. Anderson held up one hand to silence her, and he stepped closer to the chalkboard and shifted his eyeglasses. "It's an ambitious plan."

Maggie met Prescott's gaze and smiled. "It'll be spectacular."

A grumble from Mr. Anderson. "Too ambitious. Opening night is December 10, just over a month away. Twelve numbers? A Shakespearean play?"

"A short one," Maggie said. "Everyone in the cast is a professional. We're already choreographing and memorizing lines."

"Movie professionals or theater?"

"Movie."

"I've worked in theater for decades." Mr. Anderson tapped the line between the second number and act 1 of the play. "All the men are in this dance number—then immediately after, in the play. Costume changes, set changes, props—they take time. How can you keep the show under two hours? And you do have a budget, Miss Oliver."

The floor shifted beneath Maggie's feet, and her mouth flopped open. Couldn't he see how spectacular it would be?

Ria shot Maggie an apologetic look. "I've been concerned about the budget and how to procure the costumes, even if we borrow from the movie studios as Mr. Duke suggested."

Mr. Anderson planted his hands on his hips and shook his head at the board. "On opening night, we'll have admirals in attendance, city leaders, USO luminaries—luminaries who were reluctant to hire a single young lady in this role, even on a trial basis. If this show fails, many of us could lose our jobs."

A great churning rose in Maggie's stomach, and she pressed her hand to it. Her job. Grandpa's home.

"Cut it down." Mr. Anderson slashed a hand through the air, through Maggie's grand design. "I'll be in town again next Wednesday. If you can show me a sensible plan, we'll proceed. If not, we'll follow Mrs. Laverne's suggestion and put the cast on risers singing Christmas carols."

"No," Maggie whispered. "The men—they want the spectacle."

"I agree. But only a professional spectacle. I'd rather have a choir than a Keystone Cops fiasco. Understood?"

"Yes, sir." Whether a choir or a fiasco, Maggie would lose her job.

No bright side shone in Maggie's eyes after Mr. Anderson left.

Prescott knew dashed dreams, knew how the shards of them carved you up inside.

"I'm sorry, Maggie." Ria grimaced. "I—"

"No, no. You're right." Maggie waved off her assistant's apology. "I hadn't given much thought to the cost."

"Okay." Ria's jaw firmed. "Let's make a plan."

Prescott studied the board, looking for a solution.

Maggie traced a finger along the chalkboard. "I have one week to convince him this will work."

"Uh-uh." Ria shook her head. "You heard him. Cut it down or you'll be singing 'Good King Wenceslas.'"

Maggie's nose wrinkled. "I can't cut it down. It'll be simple and boring."

The numbers and costumes and songs ran through Prescott's head, heavy and encumbered. "Don't think simple. Think streamlined. A streamlined locomotive has sleek lines. Nothing slows it down. Streamline your show, and the idea will fly."

"Streamlined?" The wrinkles in her nose smoothed into something closer to acceptance.

"Yes," Ria said. "Streamline your sets. One backdrop for the whole show."

"But—"

"I see it," Prescott said. "Add a few props."

"I suppose . . ."

"Everyone!" Ria strode around the room like a train conductor. "Over here. Maggie needs your help. Unless you want to sing in a glee club, we need to streamline this show."

Footsteps and protests closed in around them.

Prescott analyzed the board. "Maggie, Mr. Anderson is concerned about the quantity of acts, but we've all learned movie scripts, with songs and dances, in less time than this. We can pull these acts together."

"I know we can." Defiance and confidence sparked in the blue of her eyes.

Prescott ran a finger on the line between numbers. "His main concern is the transitions. Here, the men are in top hat and tails. Right after, we're in Shakespearean garb. Since I need to change too, I can't serve as emcee to cover the transition."

The defiance leaked out. "Oh no."

"What if we wear one costume for the whole show?"

"Oh no," Maggie said.

"We can't do that," Vi said. "How could we dance in those heavy long dresses?"

"Yeah," Freddie said. "Besides, the fellows want to see some leg."

"But not ours." His twin brother, Ferdy, slapped his thigh. "I'm not prancing around in those silly pantaloons."

Greta sprang to the chalkboard, peeked on the opposite side, then spun it around. "May I draw, Maggie? I'm good with costumes."

Despite her dazed appearance, Maggie waved for the redhead to proceed.

"Skirts for the gals, above the knee. Trousers for the guys." Greta sketched a feminine form on the board.

Prescott nodded. "What if the costumes had a Shakespearean *look* about them?"

Light dawned through the haze in Maggie's eyes. "The V-shaped waistline—the Basque waistline. Those full sleeves gathered above the elbow with a ribbon."

"Yes. Scoop neckline, fitted bodice, flared skirt for movement." Greta's chalk flew across the board. "Red velvet dress, white sleeves, red ribbons. Add sequins for sparkle."

Maggie stepped back. "Why, that—that's cute."

"Black trousers for the men?" Prescott said.

"Yes." Greta dashed off a masculine figure. "White shirt, the same sleeves, green ribbons."

"And that vest the men wear." Freddie stroked his chest. "What's it called?"

Ferdy whapped his brother in the arm. "Jerkin."

"Who're you calling a jerk?"

"The vest is called a jerkin." Ferdy whapped him again. "And *I'm* calling you a jerk."

Greta drew the jerkin. "Green velvet. High round neck, a *V* at the waist, extensions over the shoulders."

"Oh!" Vi pointed to the men's sketch. "When Viola is dressing as Cesario, I can wear the green jerkin over my red dress. The audience knows Cesario is a woman in man's clothing—only the characters are fooled. This would play into the joke."

It would. Simply by slipping on one piece of clothing. "What do you think, Maggie?"

Her gaze darted between the male and female figures, wonder growing with each dart. Then she looked Prescott full in the face. "I think a streamlined locomotive is a thing of beauty."

So was Maggie Oliver.

THURSDAY, NOVEMBER 4, 1943

As Frank Sebastian called off measurements of the Old Globe stage, Maggie wrote them down.

Smaller than she remembered. To adapt, she'd need to streamline the large dance numbers.

Now that she'd accepted the idea—and the necessity—of streamlining, she kept finding other ways to do it.

Prescott's idea, and it was excellent. He was so clever. And calming. And humble and generous and even more of a gentleman than she'd realized. Her longtime crush had merit.

"Miss Oliver?"

Maggie blinked. "Yes?"

Frank grinned at her. He was repeating himself, wasn't he? "Ready to look backstage?"

"I am." Mr. Anderson expected a plan, and she was determined to offer a whole flock of details.

Behind the curtains, Maggie sketched the space on her clipboard.

"You can stash props here," Frank said. "A rack for costume parts there."

Yes, hats or scarves or Vi's jerkin. "You must have lots of theater experience."

He chuckled. "Only from the audience. My fiancée—she loved theater. Dragged me to every movie and show that came to our little town."

Maggie smiled at the fondness on the young man's face. "Sounds like a good match."

"It was." Ripples raced across his brow.

"Was?"

"She's gone and disappeared." He dipped his head to one side. "Nothing sinister. Nothing cruel on her part. I don't blame her."

"What do you mean?"

Frank trudged back onto the stage. "I joined the Navy waiting for her to finish school. By the time she did, I'd shipped out to the Pacific. In January of '42, my ship was sunk. But the retreat from the East Indies was so chaotic, it took months to get word to my folks that I'd survived. All Vernice knew was that I was lost at sea."

Maggie's feet edged forward. Lost at sea . . . January 1942 . . . Frank Sebastian. "Her name's Vernice?"

"Vernice Lingenfelter." Frank sent her a wobbly smile and plodded down the steps. "My folks said she was heartbroken, up and left town. No trace of her."

How horrible. She followed him off the stage. "But her family—surely, they—"

"No kin. She and her mama were all alone in town, running from someone. Vernice never would say. Her mama died her sophomore year, and friends took Vernice in."

"You have no idea where she went?" Maggie's voice came out breathless.

"No idea whatsoever."

Maggie did. She'd already heard this tale.

From the other side.

From Violet Lane.

Which sounded suspiciously like a stage name.

Maggie followed Frank Sebastian up the aisle. Now she knew where she'd heard his name. Vi's fiancé, lost at sea.

A gasp flew from Maggie's mouth. In *Twelfth Night*, Viola and Sebastian each thought the other lost at sea after a shipwreck.

Another gasp. Even their names!

In the middle of the aisle, Maggie turned in a slow circle. A reunion . . . onstage . . . on opening night. A tearjerker of a finale.

A finale sure to stir the hearts of admirals and city leaders and USO luminaries.

More importantly, a reunion that would bring happiness to two dear people.

"Miss Oliver?" Frank called from the door to the lobby.

"Getting one last look." She dashed to the door, ducking her head so she could conceal the pleased expression on her face.

Then a grimace. Over a month until opening night. She'd have to keep Frank and Vi apart, keep a secret.

Grandpa's voice rumbled in her ear. *"If you're keeping secrets, you're meddling."*

"Hush, Grandpa," she whispered. It wasn't keeping secrets. It was a Christmas gift.

FRIDAY, NOVEMBER 5, 1943

In the Bivouac Grill in the basement of the U.S. Grant Hotel, Prescott perused a lunch menu full of items he'd never heard of before 1935.

Under the low vaulted ceiling of the dining room, only a few furtive glances had been aimed at him. Almost two weeks dining in public, and no one had come at the monster in their midst with a pitchfork.

He opened the notepad by his side, with notes for his phone

call with Melvin. His story idea, each word recorded with pain and difficulty.

Yet each word he wrote spawned a dozen more. Each line of dialogue flowed to the next. Each insight into his leading man's character blossomed into scenes.

Why had the Lord chosen him to receive the gift of this story? Why hadn't the idea gone to a real writer?

It had been given to him.

As had the USO show.

At the club, he'd enjoyed a morning of creativity, camaraderie, and conversation. How he'd missed it all.

The morning had been spent streamlining choreography to make the dances easier to learn.

Maggie's cheerful determination buoyed all around her. Yet her focus on the plan never blinded her to others. The struggles with lines. The snide comments between rivals. The show-off who hogged center stage. Maggie soothed egos and hurt feelings and frustrations.

"Are you ready to order, monsieur?" an older waiter said in a French accent.

"I am, thank you. I'll have the chicken à la King."

"Oui, monsieur."

A portly gentleman approached the table. "Telephone for Mr. Prescott Duke."

Prescott's heart jolted. Melvin had returned the call he'd placed this morning. With a quick prayer, he grabbed his notepad and followed the concierge upstairs and to the bank of telephone booths in the lobby.

His breath came out jittery, so he summoned his acting experience to sound more confident than he felt. "Melvin?"

"Press! Great to hear your voice. How's the USO treating you?"

"Enjoying every minute. It'll be a swell show."

"Great. So, what's up?"

This wasn't the time to say he wanted to do more USO shows, nor to mention his upcoming performance in the naval hospital. Any distractions would chew away at his tiny morsel of courage.

One more deep breath. "I called because I have an idea for a screenplay."

"A screenplay?" A quiet cuss. "How many times—"

"I know. Every actor thinks he can write. Every actor is wrong. But this is different."

"Every actor says that."

Prescott puffed out a breath. "I can't describe how the story came to me. All I know is Charles Anthony is here, in my head, and I need to tell his story."

"Press . . ." A growl rumbled over the line.

Prescott gripped the receiver harder and read his pitch from his notepad. "Charles Anthony had it all. Important job, impressive house, beautiful family, but one tragic act—"

"No, Press. Don't. It's been told. It's been told a million times and by—no offense—by actual screenwriters."

"But this story—"

"No. This story—you've got to put it out of your head. Find a gym and a punching bag and beat it out of your head."

Prescott squeezed his eyes shut. "What if I'm right? What if it's a phenomenal story?"

Melvin fell silent, then sighed. "I'll be honest. Even if you could write it, the studio wouldn't want you to. You've heard about television. After the war, it'll be big. Huge. All those older films sitting in vaults—the studios plan to sell television rights. There's money in it. But not if you tarnish your image."

Prescott drew back his chin. "How would writing tarnish my image?"

"Come on, Press. Everyone remembers you as a handsome and debonair star. The studio needs to keep that image sharp to sell those film rights."

"My scars." Prescott's voice rasped over his throat. "You think they'll scar my image."

"In this business, image is everything. You know that. Why do you think the studio clamped down on the press after your accident? Sure, at first it was good publicity—the heroic star. But when it became clear you'd be scarred . . ."

Burning in his chest, his face, his hands.

"I'm sorry, Press." And Melvin sounded truly sorry. "I let you do this USO show against my better judgment. But a screenplay? Put it out of your head."

How could he put the story out of his head when God had put it in?

FOUR

On the fourth day of Christmas my true love sent to me . . .
four calling birds.

SATURDAY, NOVEMBER 6, 1943

Sitting in the Little Theater, Maggie tried to follow the scene in the script, but how could she when Prescott and Vi were so riveting?

After only the slightest coaching from Maggie on pronouncing the more obscure words, Prescott had found the music and rhythm of the language all on his own.

And Vi . . . she glowed. Prescott glowed right back at her.

Such chemistry on the screen was magnificent. On the stage—glorious.

So why did Maggie's heart twist? She couldn't be jealous. She'd never been that sort, and she was far too practical to think a star like Prescott would stoop down to a former ensemble dancer.

What was that uncomfortable twisting?

For Frank, surely. Pining for his Vernice, not knowing she was right here in San Diego. Pining for him.

How magnificently glorious it would be when they reunited.

The scene ended, and Prescott and Vi turned to Maggie.

She applauded. "Brava! Bravo! Keep bringing these scenes to life, and you'll make those sailor boys fall in love with Shakespeare."

Vi blushed. "Thank you. Is that all for today?"

"It is." Maggie rearranged her portfolio. "I'll see you Monday."

"Bye now." Vi grabbed her bag and dashed out of the theater.

Prescott's gaze followed the blonde out the door, then he turned to Maggie. "How long was Vi in Hollywood?"

Maggie stood and straightened the jacket of her gray suit. "A few months. I danced with her in her first picture and her second. Then I joined the USO, and she followed soon after."

Prescott stepped off the stage with a frown. "If she'd stuck around longer, she might have made it big. She has that certain . . ."

"Presence."

"Yes. More than beauty or talent—she draws you." Prescott tapped his hand over his heart.

Maggie also saw it in Vi. "Maybe after the war."

"I might be able to help her." He picked up his suit jacket draped over the back of a chair. "I may not be acting in Hollywood now, but I got along well with producers and directors."

"That would be marvelous. I'd love to see her dream come true."

"Me too." He gave her a smile, shy and hopeful, and he slipped on his jacket. "Any plans tonight? Taking your grandpa to the movies again?"

"Tonight's date is with a stack of dirty dishes in the USO kitchen." Maggie laughed at the confusion on Prescott's face. "Mrs. Laverne doesn't like having us here, so I volunteered to help at tonight's dance. Apparently I'm not to be trusted with our impressionable servicemen, but I can be trusted with the dishes."

Prescott did up his buttons with difficulty. "I'm sorry she treats you like that."

Maggie restrained herself from helping him. "How about you? What are your plans?"

"Dinner at the hotel. Then I'll read, I guess." Even on the unscarred side, his smile looked flat.

Poor man was lonely. She gave him a teasing smile. "If you're desperate, you can help in the kitchen."

His eyebrows sprang high. "You think they'd take me? I'm sorry. That sounded . . ."

Lonely. Humble. Adorable. "It sounds generous."

He stared at his hands. "I can't do much with these. They aren't capable hands anymore."

"But they're willing hands. Come on. We'll find something for you."

His grin exploded, lighting the room, and he followed her out of the theater.

In the hallway, Maggie edged to the wall to let a group of sailors pass. "Mrs. Laverne may be crabby, but she and her staff and volunteers do wonderful things here. The guests play billiards, eat at the soda fountain, swim in the pool, and make 'talk-a-letter' records to send home. The USO helps them see the sights, and they provide religious materials for all faiths. It truly is a home away from home."

Prescott peeked in a room they passed. "Woodworking?"

Maggie doubled back. The smell of sawdust met her, and half a dozen servicemen worked with a white-haired civilian.

The older gentleman beckoned to them. "Come on in. We're making birdhouses."

A freckle-faced Marine inspected his work. "Not sure my wife will think much of this."

"She'll love it," Maggie said, "because you made it for her."

"Whatcha waiting for?" The older gentleman beckoned again.

An idea spun into Maggie's head. "Say, are you looking for project ideas?"

"Always." He brushed sawdust off his apron and joined her and Prescott in the doorway. "Only so many birdhouses the fellows can make."

"I can't even make one," the Marine said with a lament in his voice.

"Props," Prescott said to Maggie.

"Exactly." She extended her hand to the carpenter. "I'm Maggie Oliver with USO-Camp Shows. We're putting on a Christmas show, and we need some wooden props."

"Herb Canfield." He gave her hand a hearty shake. "Tell me more."

"My assistant is having a difficult time finding craftsmen. The war, you know."

"I've got the craftsmen, the tools. I could help you design the pieces."

"That would be marvelous. We'd provide the materials—or the money for them. It's in my budget." She slid a smile to Prescott. "Ria will love this."

His smile slid right into hers. "Saving money."

A lanky sailor set down his saw. "You mean our work would be up on stage?"

"Wouldn't that be swell?" The Marine patted his birdhouse. "I could tell the fellows, 'I made that.'"

Maggie nodded to Mr. Canfield. "Are you here Monday morning? I'll put together a list of pieces, and we can talk about supplies."

"I'm here all day, miss." He saluted with a lopsided grin.

"To say, 'I made that.'" Prescott leaned against the doorjamb with a pensive look on his face. "Gives you a sense of purpose, doesn't it? You did something that mattered."

"Yeah, that's it." The Marine's frown at his birdhouse turned into a satisfied smile.

Prescott's pensiveness firmed into conviction.

Warmth swirled in Maggie's chest. She was doing something that mattered too. This was more than a show. She was also helping this extraordinary man find his place again.

SUNDAY, NOVEMBER 7, 1943

"Out of the way, Duke," a patient called from his bed. "I want to see the four canaries."

In a cavernous ward in what had once been the Natural History Museum, Prescott chuckled and stepped to the side, still crooning "I Had the Craziest Dream," and he ushered his four backup singers to the forefront.

Greta, Carol, Nan, and Barbara swayed to the music and sang in harmony.

Dozens of men in pajamas sat up taller in their double-deck bunks to get a better look. Confined to bed, these patients couldn't attend the show at the Old Globe, but Prescott hoped to bring bits of the show to them.

He edged around the girls, not to take center stage but to lead them down the aisle. The girls followed, twirling and gliding, while Prescott met the gaze of each man he passed.

His hands burned and itched from washing dishes the night before, but he wouldn't trade it for a thing.

How pretty Maggie had looked with her sleeves rolled up, an apron about her slender waist, suds on her chin, chatting and laughing as if he were any other man.

As if he were more than a scar. More than a star.

When he'd inserted himself into her evening, he'd sounded pathetic. But Maggie hadn't slammed the door on him. She'd pulled him right through that door.

If his life were different, if he had a future to offer, he would pursue her.

For the last verse, Prescott led his musical procession back down the aisle to the door. They took their bows and the girls blew kisses, while the patients whooped and whistled.

Lieutenant Parkinson, the Navy nurse who served as their guide, waited at the door. "Thank you so much. Are you ready to leave?"

"Do you have a burn ward?" The words came out before he could stop them.

"You don't want to—" Her pale face reddened, then she touched her own cheek. "I'm sorry, sir."

"That's quite all right. And yes, I want to. That is, if it's all right with you, ladies. A burn ward isn't very—"

"Of course it's all right." Barbara nodded her head of dark blonde curls. "We joined the USO to entertain the troops. All of them."

"All right, then." Lieutenant Parkinson led them down a hallway floored with tile, up a staircase, and into another ward with dozens of men, most bound in pressure bandages, their burned limbs elevated to reduce swelling.

Prescott's breath snagged in his throat. The smells. The sights. The groans.

"Gentlemen, may I have your attention?" the nurse called out. "I have a special treat for you from the USO. None other than movie star Prescott Duke and four lovely singers to entertain you."

Prescott was supposed to thank the lieutenant, greet the patients, and introduce the song, but his vocal cords protested.

Not a song. Not yet.

"I've been here." His words came out cramped, and he shook his head to loosen them. "I have been here. Not this ward, but one just like it. I enlisted. I wanted to fight. I never got the chance. My bus to training camp got in an accident, caught on fire. And I ended up here."

Prescott wandered down the aisle. "I know the heat that won't go away. I know the stench of burned flesh, the sting of raw meat, the constriction of scars, the loss of fingers. I know the stares, the averted gazes, the pity. I know the loss of relationships."

"My girl . . ." a sailor bound in white sobbed out the words.

Prescott's heart burned far more than his face ever had. "It feels like the end, doesn't it? We don't look the same. We may not be able to do the things we love. May not be able to perform our old jobs. Simple daily tasks are painful, difficult."

Silence filled the ward. Grief. Loss. Fear.

It had consumed Prescott's heart for almost two years.

He knew it as truth in his own life, but he loathed it in these men's lives, wanted to refute it, and that burning in his heart seared its way up his throat.

Prescott swept his arm around the room as if he could wipe out the lie. "This is not the end. Your mind still works. Your heart still beats. Your character—why, it's stronger than before, isn't it? Let it grow even stronger. As Shakespeare said, 'In nature there's no blemish but the mind, none can be call'd deform'd but the unkind.'"

"So true," one of the ladies murmured.

Prescott marched down the aisle, pointing at each man. "Let this trial build your compassion for the hurting, build your determination to persevere, build your strength, your patience. Let this heat burn off any arrogance that hinders you and let it humble you in the best possible way."

In the slits of bandages, eyes brightened.

Prescott's voice built. "With your mind, your heart, and your character, you can do great things. This world is a mess. We need you. As you are. Burned, scarred, disfigured—and smart and strong and compassionate. We need you."

His words stopped, and they settled down and filtered in.

Filtered into his own heart too.

A sniffle from the doorway, and Carol and Greta wiped their eyes with hankies.

Prescott raised a self-conscious smile. "Honest, fellows, we came to make music, not speeches. Ladies, how about 'Blue Skies'?"

Four heads bobbled, and hankies disappeared into pockets.

Prescott gave them a count of four and launched in, singing of blue skies and bluebirds. Of joy and hope driving away the blue days.

"This story—you've got to put it out of your head," Melvin had told him.

But Maggie had told him, *"Write a new script for your life."*

Prescott had always been a storyteller. He knew movie people and the movie industry. Screenwriting wouldn't shine limelight on his scarred face to tarnish the image in the public's mind. He'd just be a name in the credits.

And he might not be educated, but what made the best writing? Knowledge of people and of the difficulties of life. That he had in spades.

The smells remained in the ward. The sights.

But the heaviness had lifted, because Prescott had employed his story.

More than anything, he wanted these men—and so many others like them—to move on with their lives. To help them do so, Prescott had to move on himself.

WEDNESDAY, NOVEMBER 10, 1943

"That's the plan." With Ria beside her, Maggie smiled at Mr. Anderson across the table in a meeting room at the YMCA. And at Mrs. Laverne to Mr. Anderson's left.

Mr. Anderson reviewed the papers Ria had typed, listing each number, with cast members, music, props, and costs—and listing what would happen in the intervals between numbers.

The plan was streamlined, yet contained spectacle, music, and laughs. And it remained true to what she and Prescott had envisioned that morning in Balboa Park.

Mr. Anderson moved his finger down the paper. "This is much improved."

"Thank you, sir." Maggie let her smile beam. "The entire cast worked together on every aspect." Especially Prescott.

Mrs. Laverne sniffed. "The whole thing is silly and overblown."

If only she'd heard some of the ideas tossed out in jest—like when Freddie and Ferdy suggested doing bird calls.

"It's still too complex." Mr. Anderson sat back and scooted

his glasses higher. "You've solved the problem of transitions, but you have too many numbers and a Shakespeare play, to boot."

Dimples of concern pocked Mrs. Laverne's full cheeks. "As I said, it would be easier and more reverential to sing carols."

Mr. Anderson grumbled, and his chin wagged in the way of a man about to agree.

Panic ripped through Maggie's chest, but she glued on a confident smile. "Sir, I know we can do this. The cast is hard at work, making great progress. There are only four big dance numbers. The rest are small acts—solos, comedy bits, acrobatics."

Ria folded her hands on top of the table. "Remember, sir. You hired Miss Oliver to put on a big Christmas show, not a sing-along. USO-Camp Shows is known for quality productions, and that's what our servicemen expect—and deserve—especially so far from home."

"Yes, Mrs. Fernandez," he said. "They deserve quality, not a fiasco."

"It won't be a fiasco," Maggie said.

"If only you could guarantee it. No, I—"

"How about this?" Ria's dark eyes flashed. "How about a—a trial performance?"

"A trial?" Maggie said at the same time as Mr. Anderson.

Ria motioned to Maggie. "What if Miss Oliver has the cast run through the show for you next week? If it's coming along well, she can proceed. If you're still concerned, we can do the sing-along."

Maggie's mouth flopped open. The show wouldn't be ready next week. It would be ready by opening night. All shows were like that.

A smug glint shone in Mrs. Laverne's light blue eyes.

"Excellent idea," Mr. Anderson said. "Don't worry, Miss Oliver.

I don't expect perfection, just proof that it will work. I know the costumes and sets won't be ready, and the actors can use scripts if needed. A week from today."

"One week?" Maggie's voice sounded thin and hopeless.

"One week," Mr. Anderson said. "Plenty of time to pull the essentials together."

Mrs. Laverne's smile returned to cherubic. "Plenty of time to switch to a proper choir concert."

Mr. Anderson looked to Maggie with an expectant smile.

Only one answer was expected. "Yes, sir. I'll do my best."

Two decades before, Ma had turned her back on Prescott. He refused to turn his back on others.

If his story could help, he had to write it.

Wearing a sports shirt and swim trunks, Prescott carried a towel and his attaché case across Ocean Beach in the warm air. Cool sand threaded between his toes.

His aimlessness was far uglier than his scars, and he had to kill it before it killed him, had to overcome it if he wanted others to overcome.

Since his performance in the hospital on Sunday, he'd argued with himself. He was too busy with the show to write. He had no business writing. And *how* could he write? Typewriters were only available for purchase with a certificate from the ration board, which Prescott would never qualify for.

Besides, the thought of pounding keys with the fried nubs of his fingers was even less appealing than using the fat pencils they'd given him while recovering in the hospital.

Prescott passed a group of mothers seated on towels with a passel of tots laughing and squabbling and digging in the sand.

He found an isolated spot right before the sand turned from fluffy to slick, and he spread out his towel.

Four seagulls dove toward the water, calling to each other.

"Why am I doing this?" he asked the gulls. "You think I'm doing this to impress Maggie, don't you? Show her I'm not an idle loafer?"

Sitting cross-legged on his towel, he opened his attaché case and pulled out a sheet of paper and a pencil meant for a first grader. Maggie had given the men the morning off. She had a meeting, then was working with the ladies on their solo acts.

He'd rather be with her than facing a fat pencil and a thin piece of paper.

A pale blue sky spread above him, streaked with airy white clouds and contrails from the Naval Air Station on North Island. Gray-blue waves trimmed in foam slapped the golden sand.

"Why am I doing this?" he asked the waves.

The first scene would be heart-wrenching, but it took place at sea, on Charles Anthony's luxurious yacht, so sitting at the ocean's edge felt right.

Now Prescott knew that Charles was a wealthy politician. He'd invited four powerful men out on his yacht. Pillars of the community. Admired and respected by all. Their wives. His own wife and children. A sumptuous party to raise money and prestige and influence.

His captain warned him about a coming storm. His wife begged him to postpone.

Charles insisted.

The yacht was lost with all aboard—except Charles.

In the ensuing scandal, he lost his seat in the House and his positions in companies and committees and philanthropies.

He'd lived for his image. Many souls died for his image. Then he lost that image.

All he had left was money and a beautiful empty house.

Prescott groaned, and his head sagged to his chest. That was all he had left too. His image had been destroyed by scars, not scandal, but destroyed it remained.

Who was he now? He certainly wasn't Joe Prescott anymore. He couldn't go back and didn't want to. But who would he become?

And who would Charles Anthony become? For Charles to move forward, Prescott Duke had to move pencil over paper. So he did.

EXT. CHARLES ANTHONY'S YACHT AT SEA—CONTINUOUS

Five wealthy couples mingle and sip champagne. The yacht rocks in a rising wind. Smiles turn to nervous glances. Champagne sloshes to the deck.

FELICIA ANTHONY approaches CHARLES, holding back her hair in the wind.

FELICIA

Charles? Don't you think we should turn back? The weather . . .

CHARLES

It's fine. The captain worries too much. I tell you, Felicia, I'm so close to—

Prescott winced and paused to stretch his hand. Holding the pencil between thumb and his two remaining fingers—middle and ring on his right hand—was difficult enough without the pain and stiffness.

"Why am I doing this?" he asked the pencil.

Perhaps as he walked alongside Charles Anthony and helped him figure out his purpose, Prescott would figure out his purpose too.

God's love was more than enough, but God had created him for meaningful work and relationships. Without those, Prescott had been wasting away, and Charles would too.

In this story, Prescott would take Charles low, then help him rise.

The breeze ruffled Prescott's hair. "Lord, help me rise too."

FIVE

On the fifth day of Christmas my true love sent to me . . .
five gold rings.

SATURDAY, NOVEMBER 13, 1943

At the streetcar terminal outside Balboa Park's eastern gate, Maggie chatted with Frank Sebastian in front of a truck, while Ria checked off cast members as they boarded from the back.

Frank had procured two canvas-covered trucks to corral the two dozen civilians on naval property. For Maggie, it helped blind Frank and Vi to each other's presence. If Frank and Vi did sight each other, Maggie would see it as God's way of overriding her plans. But surely the Lord wanted a romantic reunion as much as she did.

"That's everyone," Ria called to Maggie.

"Thank you. Come ride up front with the yeoman." Portfolio in hand, Maggie climbed into the back of the truck filled with men and women singing "Winter Wonderland" on a hazy—but hardly wintry—morning.

The truck rumbled through the gate and down Laurel Street,

and the canvas formed an arched framework around the park's grand exposition buildings.

Today would be the first of only three rehearsals in the Old Globe and the last full rehearsal before the trial performance for Mr. Anderson.

Maggie's stomach tensed. Only four days to go.

In a few minutes, the trucks turned in front of the Museum of Man and its soaring California Tower and parked outside the theater.

"Stay here until the theater door is unlocked. The Navy doesn't trust us." To the laughter of the cast, Maggie held up one hand in mock warning and climbed out of the truck.

While Frank unlocked the door, Maggie repeated her order at the second truck—partly to keep her lovebirds apart and partly to convince the Navy that show people could in fact be trusted.

Frank gave her a thumbs-up, and Maggie beckoned to the cast in the second truck. As the players entered the theater, Frank led Ria toward his office in the administration building so they could schedule the shows and the busing of sailors and soldiers and Marines from the many bases in San Diego. And from the convalescent hospital wards.

Eyeing the retreating forms of Frank and Ria, Maggie strolled to the first truck.

Vi hopped out, her attention fixed on the theater. "It's charming."

"It is." Maggie smiled at her friend's delight and in her own delight at the joyful opening night awaiting that friend.

Inside, she showed the cast backstage to the dressing rooms to change into practice clothes, then she set up camp in the third row of the theater and organized her papers.

After the cast came onstage, Maggie clapped to get their attention. "This morning, we won't practice songs or routines or scenes from the play. We'll just work on blocking. Who moves where and when? Where will you store props or costume accessories? I'd like to block the whole show before lunch, then do two full run-throughs this afternoon. Let's get started. Everyone exit either stage left or stage right—wherever you are for 'Winter Wonderland.'"

The cast parted like oil and vinegar and disappeared into the wings.

"The band stops playing," Maggie said. "The curtains open, and Prescott enters."

He did so, wearing brown trousers and a short-sleeved sports shirt of autumn gold. In the sunshine, would the color bring out flecks of gold in his brown eyes?

Maggie shook herself. She was a director, not a fan.

"Emcee talk, winking, smiling, more emcee talk." Prescott stopped center stage as the cast's laughter drifted from backstage. "Introduce our partridge in a pear tree."

"Perfect." Maggie loved seeing him relaxed and comfortable.

As Vi entered, Prescott exited with a grand gesture to his leading lady.

"'White Christmas,'" Vi said, rocking back and forth as if swinging, and then flitted away.

Prescott returned. "Maggie, perhaps I should sing 'Winter Wonderland' after all, since the blocking depends on the lyrics."

A moment to think, and she nodded. At this point in the show, she wanted to feature the entire cast, but the small stage had created a challenge.

At Barbara's suggestion, two couples at a time would tap

dance onstage, perform vignettes corresponding to the lyrics, and exit, some couples crossing left to right upstage, others right to left downstage, creating circular motion around Prescott as he sang.

"When I clap three times, stop so we can find your marks," Maggie called. "Ready? One, two, three, four."

Prescott launched into the song with his voice of midnight blue velvet, rich and sonorous. Two couples sashayed out from opposite sides of the stage, taps clicking the floorboards. Maggie clapped three times and directed the couples to create a pleasing diagonal line across the stage. She clapped again, and the number resumed.

The routine was rough, but vignettes played out with Jack as a snowman and Albert as Parson Brown, and the number promised to be fun and playful.

As each couple passed Prescott, he gave them wistful looks, as if a lonely heart waiting for his own turtle dove, until at last Vi entered. She and Prescott twirled together, singing the final chorus in harmony, Vi's hair flying in a golden wing as her head lolled back in bliss.

If only Maggie could dance with Prescott like that.

She puffed out a breath, puffed away the silly flash of jealousy.

But was it jealousy? Or concern for three friends?

How could Vi resist Prescott? Or Prescott resist Vi? If they fell in love, what would happen when Vi was reunited with Frank?

Such potential for heartbreak.

Maggie winced as the couple sang the final notes. Perhaps she shouldn't delay that reunion. Or did her hastiness stem from a desire to keep Prescott for herself—as if that were even possible?

After Vi floated offstage, Prescott added a trace of mischief to his smile. "Introduce *Twelfth Night*. Say that Shakespeare will turn them from sailors to gentlemen."

Maggie laughed, as all worries melted in the warmth of his smile.

The cool air felt good, especially on the left side of Prescott's face, since scar tissue couldn't sweat.

Ria had brought a cart from the mess with a coffee urn and a stack of deviled ham sandwiches, and the cast lounged on benches in the plaza, enjoying their lunch.

Well, most were enjoying it. Albert separated the pieces of bread and wrinkled his long nose at the pinkish spread inside. "I know why deviled ham isn't rationed. No one wants it."

"'*Pourquoi*, my dear knight?'" Freddie quoted his character in *Twelfth Night*, Sir Toby Belch.

Albert assumed the empty-headed expression of his own character, Sir Andrew Aguecheek. "'What is *pourquoi*? Do or not do? I would I had bestowed that time in the tongues, that I have in fencing, dancing, and bear-baiting.'"

Prescott joined the chuckling. He had missed this sort of camaraderie. In less than two months, he would miss it again.

No, he wouldn't, because he was determined to rejoin the world of the living.

On the far side of the plaza, Maggie sat facing the broad tiled dome and tall tower of the adjacent building.

Prescott tilted his head. It wasn't like her to be alone.

If only he could sit with her. If only he had the guts to ask her out.

He tilted his head in the other direction. Why not? He was vanquishing the aimlessness that had held him back. He'd written fifteen pages in his screenplay, and the story grew in his mind, deepened, compelled him to write more. When Melvin read it, he would surely approve. To relieve his agent's concerns about image, Prescott would remind him that writers' faces weren't plastered on movie posters. And he could always use a pen name.

Prescott swallowed the last bite of sandwich and returned his cup and plate to the cart.

He'd give Maggie an easy escape in case his scars were a bigger barrier to romance than they were to friendship. He'd ask her plans for the evening. If she was taking her grandpa to the movies, he'd weasel an invitation.

Not the most romantic of dates, but he simply wanted to spend time with her.

The sun had dissolved the morning haze, surely for the sole purpose of lighting up Maggie's brown hair.

Prescott sat beside her and rested his elbows on the back of the bench. "Hi there."

She looked up from a letter in her hands and brightened. "Hello."

The brightening emboldened him. "Hiding from the five-ring circus?" He tipped his head to the cast.

"Five ring?" Then Maggie laughed. "Five gold rings. Clever."

"What are you reading?"

"A letter from Rose, my little sister. Well, my mother wrote it, but it's from Rose."

Prescott fought a frown. What did she mean?

Maggie stroked the stationery. "Rose can't read or write. She—

she had meningitis at the age of three, and she'll always be three inside."

"I'm sorry."

Pain crimped her mouth, but then she smiled at him. "Thank you, but Rose is a light in our lives. Listen to this—Rose says she rolls bandages at the Red Cross three times a week. I suspect the Red Cross ladies save all the bandages just for her."

Prescott rubbed his thumbs to his remaining fingers. Rose didn't let her infirmity stop her from aiding the war effort. "She sounds remarkable."

"She is. You might get to meet her. She's coming to San Diego with my parents for Christmas. I know, I know. As the posters say, 'Millions of troops are on the move. Is your trip necessary?' Tell that to my father. He's a lawyer. He'll find a way."

The more he heard about the Oliver family, the more he wanted to meet them. "I'm sure you'll be glad to see them."

"Yes." But a virtual cloud snuffed the sun in her blue-sky eyes.

Why? Was she embarrassed by Rose?

No, she seemed proud of her sister, which aligned with Maggie's compassionate character. Was Rose's infirmity the reason for Maggie's compassion?

The cloud remained, so he nudged her with an elbow. "What's the matter?"

She heaved a sigh. "It's my grandfather. His savings are running low, so I asked Papa to help, not knowing he was already helping—and that Papa owns Grandpa's house. Now Papa wants to sell and move Grandpa to Iowa. But I'm making enough to meet our expenses now." Another sigh. "I made a mess of things. Grandpa says I was meddling."

"Were you?" Prescott kept his voice soft.

She made a face. "Maybe. I was trying to help. Now Grandpa won't even let me write to Papa about this, but I know I could convince him." Earnestness pulsed in her expression.

Prescott shrugged. "But if it's your grandfather's house . . ."

"I know." She folded the letter. "If I don't keep this job, it's all over."

"You'll keep this job. You're doing wonderful work." More than anything, he wanted to take her hand—in *his*? What was he thinking? Not yet.

But he could ask her out, and he saw a transition between scenes, between her grandfather's woes and the evening's plans. "You're very fond of your grandfather, aren't you?"

"I am. He's . . ." She squinted at the path ahead.

Ria approached with Petty Officer Sebastian.

Maggie sprang to her feet and clapped her hands. "All right, everyone. Time to practice. Put your dishes on the cart and head inside. On the double."

"Yes, ma'am." Much laughing and saluting and clicking of heels.

Maggie rushed over to Vi. "Please make sure the props are in place for act 1. Barbara, would you please take care of Vi's dishes for her?"

Prescott groaned and stood. He had one last chance to ask Maggie out, and he came up behind her and tapped her shoulder.

She faced him, smiled at him, and he opened his mouth.

Her gaze jerked past him, and her eyes widened. "Excuse me." With a brilliant smile, Maggie brushed past him and over to the yeoman.

Turned her back on him.

Prescott grimaced and marched toward the theater. If Maggie

preferred a sunny, smooth-skinned sailor to a melancholy Hollywood has-been, who could blame her?

MONDAY, NOVEMBER 15, 1943

Women bustled about the USO gymnasium, and Maggie stood in the doorway, mouth agape.

Holding a reel of red crepe paper, Mrs. Laverne gave Maggie an innocent smile. "May I help you?"

Maggie throttled back her annoyance and echoed the woman's fake smile. "I assume we can rehearse in here this morning—as scheduled."

Mrs. Laverne pursed her lips. "There must be a misunderstanding. We have a dance in here tonight. I'm sorry you didn't see it on the schedule."

How could Maggie see what wasn't there? But she could indeed see the smirk on the older woman's face.

In the hallway, the ten men and three ladies in *Twelfth Night* gave her quizzical looks.

"We'll go to the Little Theater, then," Maggie said.

Mrs. Laverne clucked her tongue. "If you'd looked at the schedule, you would have seen we're holding lectures in there all day."

And if Mrs. Laverne had looked at the schedule, she would have seen the cast was rehearsing in the gym. But no good would come of saying so.

"What's wrong?" Prescott asked in that gorgeous voice.

Maggie refused to be riled as Mrs. Laverne intended. "We can't practice in the gym today. Or the Little Theater."

"But the trial performance is on Wednesday." Panic shimmered in Vi's voice. "This is our last day to work on *Twelfth Night*."

Maggie's head spun. Tomorrow, only the Little Theater was available, which didn't have room for the play.

Albert slapped the wall with his long-fingered hand. "We have to cancel."

"We can't." Maggie's voice trembled. "We need to run through the scenes, rehearse the blocking."

Prescott's brow furrowed, but a soothing steadiness rested in his gaze. "Your boss said we could use scripts. That will help."

Not if her players banged around like bumper cars. "We'll go somewhere else."

"Where?" Carol asked. "A park?"

Too distracting, too public. "We'll go to my grandfather's house, his backyard."

Maggie herded the cast out through the lobby, onto Broadway, and down two blocks to Horton Plaza. Before long, a trolley for the No. 7 line arrived in the sage green and cream of the San Diego Electric Railway. Since more people were heading into downtown than out, there was room for all of them.

Prescott handed the driver a dollar and forty cents to cover the crowd, and he sat across the aisle from Maggie. "That was a quick solution. I'm impressed."

"Don't be." She chuckled. "Wait until Grandpa sees all these show people at his door."

And show people were . . . show people. As the trolley dinged its way up Broadway, Freddie and Ferdy sang "Who Wouldn't Love You?" with a soft-shoe routine in the aisle.

If the twins weren't identical, she would have cast them in the two main comedic roles, but with identical costumes, the audience would have been confused. Since they were slender and blond, she'd cast Ferdy as Sebastian, Viola's twin, and added a green velvet hat to Vi's and Ferdy's costumes to further the conceit that they could be mistaken for each other.

Prescott got Maggie's attention and—with a wry smile—tipped his head toward a middle-aged woman who held her magazine high to block the offense of music on the trolley.

But Maggie tipped her own head to a smiling elderly lady nodding to the beat.

The trolley wended up Park Boulevard, through Balboa Park, and onto University Avenue. When the trolley stopped at 30th Street, Maggie led everyone through the North Park neighborhood and had them wait on the sidewalk outside Grandpa's house.

"Grandpa?" Maggie stepped inside. "I have a huge favor to ask."

In his armchair, Grandpa lowered the *San Diego Union*. "Don't you have rehearsals?"

"Mrs. Laverne kicked us out. Could we practice in the backyard? No song and dance to scandalize the neighbors. Just Shakespeare."

"Well . . . sure." Grandpa laid his paper on the coffee table. "Let me clean up and—"

"No need." Maggie leaned out the front door. "Come on in."

Grandpa chuckled and pushed himself to standing with his canes to greet his guests.

Maggie introduced each as they filed through to the yard, with Prescott last in line. "Grandpa, this is—"

"Prescott Duke!" Grandpa pumped his hand heartily. "I'm Bill Curtis. Maggie's thrilled to have you in her show. We're both fans. She's taken me to every one of your pictures."

Maggie's smile stiffened. At least Grandpa hadn't asked for an autographed photo for Maggie to smooch every night.

"I'm honored, Mr. Curtis," Prescott said. "Thank you for opening your home to us."

In the yard, the men were scooting flowerpots to mark the corners of the stage. After Maggie dusted off a lawn chair, she sat down with her script.

Act 1, scene 1. Prescott stood stage left, the area designated as Duke Orsino's palace.

In his opening monologue, Prescott's wistfulness added poignancy to the duke's unrequited longing for Olivia. In the second scene, Viola stumbled onstage, shipwrecked, and learned her twin brother, Sebastian, was lost at sea. Vi's own mourning for Frank made her voice quiver.

A little over three weeks until they would be reunited, a Christmas gift and surprise party all in one. Even Grandpa couldn't fault Maggie for keeping such a secret.

Scene 3—the comedic trio of Sir Toby, Sir Andrew, and Maria. Carol possessed the wit and timing for Maria's role. If only she'd learned her lines. Maggie gave her another gentle reminder.

Then the fourth scene, between Duke Orsino and Viola disguised as Cesario. Thinking her a man, Orsino confessed his love for Olivia, but Viola was already pining for the duke.

Such palpable chemistry between Prescott and Vi. Was it based in reality?

What about Frank?

Perhaps Maggie should try to keep Prescott and Vi apart.

That would be the worst sort of meddling, the selfish sort, the jealous sort. Because her affection for Prescott grew deeper each day.

Maggie squeezed her eyes shut and prayed. Tried to listen. So difficult when she had so much to say.

"Maggie?" Prescott said. "Did we put you to sleep?"

She opened her eyes to see Prescott and Vi grinning at her. She smiled back. "Excellent. All right, scene 5. Lots of movement. Lots of humor. Let's be lively."

As the final scene finished, Prescott held Vi in his arms. Thank goodness there was no kissing in this play. He didn't miss that part of Hollywood.

Maggie rose in her dark blue suit. "Much better. That's all for today. Ladies, please be at the club tomorrow at nine o'clock sharp. Practice your lines." But she was speaking to the cast members' backs as they dispersed, chattering about plans for the evening.

Did Maggie have plans? Prescott gathered his script and bag. Frank Sebastian looked awful young for Maggie, but looks could be deceiving. And it was none of his business.

"Prescott? Vi?" Maggie beckoned them closer. "Would you like to join my grandfather and me for dinner? Just tuna casserole, I'm afraid."

"Oh." Vi's gaze skittered to the door. "I had plans with Carol."

Practicing Carol's lines, Prescott hoped.

"That's all right." Maggie's smile turned sheepish. "Prescott? Grandpa would love it."

He should leap at the chance to get a leg up on sailor boy, but why bother? Maggie cared for him only as a friend, as the star of her show. And he had planned to write after dinner. He wanted to finish the first act in his script before tomorrow's meeting with Melvin.

"I understand." Maggie's smile stretched too wide. "The hotel serves far fancier fare."

How could he disappoint her? Or himself? And he'd never tried tuna casserole. "I'd be happy to join you."

With the cast gone, Maggie motioned him inside. "I like this recipe because it's fast if I cook it on the stove. It's better baked, but at least I have all the ingredients. That's the hard part about working full time. No time to shop or cook. I'm sorry. I'm babbling."

"Not at all." He loved her babbling.

Maggie led him down a narrow hall past three shut doors, bed and bath, most likely, past the kitchen door, and into the living room, with a couch, two armchairs, a radio cabinet, and a fireplace. Compact and cozy and unlike tenements and mansions, the only homes he'd known.

"Grandpa, Prescott's staying for dinner."

"Great." The older gentleman wrestled with canes beside his armchair.

"No need to stand." Prescott took the seat Maggie showed him on an old-fashioned couch. After Maggie went to the kitchen, he smiled at Mr. Curtis. "How long have you lived here?"

"Thirty years. Worked with the builder to make this place just the way I wanted."

"Grandpa owned a hardware store. He's very handy." Maggie peeked through a window-like opening in the wall between kitchen and living room. "See? He designed this so he could talk to Grandma while she cooked. Isn't that sweet?"

"Very." Prescott's smile dipped as Mr. Curtis spun a gold wedding ring on his finger. "How long has she been gone?"

Mr. Curtis blew out a sigh. "Four years now. Tuberculosis."

"I'm sorry. You must miss her very much."

Brown eyes crowned by snowy eyebrows lifted to Prescott. "It's tougher than getting around with these things. And I hate them." He whacked one of the canes at his side.

Metal clanked on metal in the kitchen. "Tell him why you need canes, Grandpa."

"Psh. It's nothing."

"Nothing?" Maggie leaned through the window. "He was up on the roof fixing shingles."

Mr. Curtis shrugged still-broad shoulders. "Needed fixing."

Maggie whirled back to work. "Broke his hip and both legs."

Mr. Curtis raised one arm and winked at Prescott. "Don't forget my wrist."

"I'm just glad you didn't break your head," Maggie called.

Prescott smiled at the teasing affection.

Mr. Curtis frowned at the ceiling. "I noticed two loose shingles the other day."

"Don't you dare." Maggie aimed an icicle of a glare through the window.

The mischief in Mr. Curtis's expression shifted to frustration.

Frustration Prescott understood. "It's difficult not doing the things you used to do."

Mr. Curtis grunted. "Hate using canes. Worse, the wheelchair. But I get by. The church ladies help me around the house, and they bring me doodads to fix. It's important for a man not to be idle."

"Grandpa . . ." Maggie winced.

"What?" He pulled his chin back. "Idleness is bad for the soul."

Prescott chuckled. "Your granddaughter's worried you'll hurt my feelings."

"Why? Acting in movies isn't idle. Although stardom can become an *idol*." He winked.

That's where Maggie got her sense of humor. "I'm afraid losing my stardom has indeed made me idle, which is—as you said—bad for the soul. I'm determined to find a way out."

"More USO shows, I hope?" Maggie said. "You're welcome in any of mine."

Nothing appealed to him more. But the need for USO shows would end with the war, which couldn't last long with the progress the Allies were making in Italy and the Pacific.

"What did you do before Hollywood?" Mr. Curtis said.

"Boxing, odd jobs, some of them illegal. Nothing to return to."

A scratching sound rose from the back of the house.

"That's Tobias, my dog." Mr. Curtis waved to the back hall. "I didn't want him getting in the way during your rehearsals. Maggie?"

She was already on her way, and soon a scrappy gray-and-white mutt danced around Mr. Curtis's knees, then Prescott's.

"Hi there. Tobias, is it?" Prescott scratched the dog behind his mismatched ears.

"Push him away if he annoys you," Mr. Curtis said.

"Never." Warmth flooded Prescott's chest. "I had a dog for a few months when I was riding the rails. Grizzled old gal. Then one morning, she didn't wake up."

"Oh, Prescott." Distress marred Maggie's sweet voice. "That's so sad. All your stories are."

He sat up taller, and his fingers stilled behind Tobias's ears. "I do have happy stories. My pa—he was the best father I could imagine. And riding the rails—I made good friends, saw the country. And I loved acting in the movies."

Peeking through the window, Maggie beamed at him.

Tobias bumped Prescott with his nose, and Prescott resumed scratching.

"And today," he murmured. Today was happy.

SIX

On the sixth day of Christmas my true love sent to me . . .
six geese a-laying.

LOS ANGELES
TUESDAY, NOVEMBER 16, 1943

Only a month earlier, Prescott had sat outside Melvin Underwood's fancy office on Wilshire Boulevard, hopeless, aimless.

Today he held an attaché case filled with hope and aim. And tomorrow he'd ask Maggie out. He'd already made dinner reservations at the Hotel del Coronado. If she was in love with Frank Sebastian, he'd rather find out now. And if she wasn't? Well, it was time.

Edna opened Melvin's door. "He'll see you now."

Melvin met him halfway across the office with a firm handshake. "Don't tell me the USO has already fired you."

"Not at all." He returned the grin. "In fact, they'd like to have me in more shows."

Melvin's broad nose wrinkled as he rounded his desk. "I'd rather you didn't."

"Since I no longer have a studio contract, I'm free." Prescott settled into the leather armchair. "I've also been performing in the naval hospital. I tell you, something good is coming of it."

Melvin blew out a long breath. "I preferred it when you were the Hollywood Hermit."

Prescott didn't. With a quick prayer for nerves, he opened his attaché case. "The USO isn't why I came today. This is." He set his script in front of his agent.

"What is it?" Melvin thumbed through the painstakingly written pages.

Prescott cleared his throat. "Act 1 of my screenplay."

Melvin chomped off a curse. "I told you—"

"You told me to get it out of my head. I did. Got it out of my head and onto paper."

Melvin's jaw dangled. "Handwritten? In pencil?"

Muscles tensed in Prescott's shoulders. "I don't have a typewriter."

"And *badly* handwritten." Melvin sat back and tossed his hands wide. "What are you thinking, Press?"

A deep breath, a deep prayer, and Prescott gave his agent a steady gaze. "It's a powerful story. You represent writers as well as actors. I know you can get this moving."

Shaking his big head, Melvin shoved the script back across the desk.

Prescott stopped him, both hands on the precious pages, both lungs pulsing air. "Please. Please read it. Out of courtesy if nothing else. Have I ever let you down?"

Melvin glowered, but then he groaned, scraped the script back toward him, and put on his reading glasses.

As Melvin read the first page, Prescott gripped the black leather of his attaché case. Melvin had lifted Prescott from poverty to fame, taught him, nurtured him, believed in him.

Melvin peeked at the second page, flopped the first page back in place, and sat back again in his chair. "You poured your heart into this. It shows."

"Thank you." But he heard heaviness in his agent's tone.

"I'm sorry, Press. I can't pitch this. It's a mess. Spelling errors, crossed-out words, almost illegible."

Prescott's breath became choppy, and he fought to compose his face.

Melvin leaned his elbows on the desk, and his gray eyebrows drew together. "I hate to say this, but you aren't a writer."

The rotten-egg stench of rejection filled his nostrils, and he sucked in a breath. "You only read one page. If you read a few more—"

"I don't have to." Melvin's voice dove low into concern, but concern girded with steel. "I work with talent all day, every day. I know it when I see it. And this?" He whapped the script. "I don't see it."

A door slammed in Prescott's head. With fumbling, aching fingers, he gathered his script, nestled it in his attaché case.

Melvin stood, went to the door, and opened it. "Remember, you have plenty of money, solid investments. You don't need to do stuff like this."

Somehow Prescott pushed himself out of the chair and left the office.

"Miss Baker is here to see you," Edna called.

"Miss Baker, what a pleasure." Melvin ushered a pretty young blonde into the office and shut the door.

Prescott stared at that door. His heart pounded.

Fourteen years old. Alone in the tenement hallway with nothing but a satchel.

What now? Where could he go? What could he do with his life?

He couldn't be a screenwriter.

Slam.

He couldn't go back to the movies.

Slam.

He refused to return to the boxing ring. To life as a hermit.

He slammed those doors himself.

Sensing Edna's curious gaze on his back, Prescott shoved out a polite goodbye and exited stage left.

Only as a movie star had he ever had any worth. Now he had none.

SAN DIEGO
WEDNESDAY, NOVEMBER 17, 1943

In the gymnasium, Maggie tried not to look at Mr. Anderson and Ria as the cast ran through the trial performance.

For the "twelve drummers drumming" curtain call, Prescott sang "The Twelve Days of Christmas," pausing after each phrase while the performers for the corresponding act came onstage, did a sample of their routine, and took their bows.

During the real show, the band's drummer would play a jazzy solo for each act. But today, they had sweet Mrs. Chester on the piano, trying to pound chords like a drummer. Since she played like a church organist, not a jazz pianist, she added to the flatness of the performance.

No one's performance had been flatter than Prescott Duke's.

"'Ten lords a-leaping . . .'" he sang.

The men ran onto the tape-bordered stage, and Freddie and Ferdy performed backflips, collided with each other, bonked heads.

"Oh no." Maggie gasped and rose halfway out of her chair.

Freddie sat on the floor, massaging his forehead. "I'm going to get a goose egg."

"First you're going to get off the stage." Ferdy tugged his twin to standing.

"'Nine ladies dancing . . .'" Prescott sang fine, acted fine, danced fine. But the spark was missing. Before the performance, he'd been quiet and glum. Had something happened?

Maggie resisted the urge to chew her thumbnail. She'd cured herself of that habit in junior high, but Prescott's downcast gaze and slumped shoulders churned her insides.

"'Six geese a-laying . . .'"

Nothing happened.

"Carol," Maggie muttered under her breath.

Barbara and Greta prodded Carol, who squealed, grabbed her top hat, dashed onto stage, and pulled an egg from her hat, echoing her magic act.

Maggie's thumbnail gravitated toward her mouth, and she gripped her hands together. That was—appropriately enough—the twelfth major missed cue in the show. Plus countless minor errors, which might or might not escape Mr. Anderson's attention.

She ventured a glance at her boss's impassive face. Not once had he even chuckled.

Why hadn't she streamlined down to a regular USO show format? Three or four acts, each performing song and dance and comedy for half an hour. Each responsible for their own performance. No interconnection.

"'Two turtle doves . . .'" Prescott extended a hand to Vi, who joined him for a twirl and a bow. Then he stepped aside and gestured to Vi, standing alone at center stage. Vi sang in her soaring soprano, "'And a partridge in a pear tree.'"

After she curtsied, the cast lined up onstage, alternating men and women—in costume, green and red would alternate in a festive way—and they sang "Happy Holiday."

At least they knew the lyrics.

What did it matter? It was over. The run-through made the Keystone Cops look like sailors on parade.

She'd lose her job. Grandpa would lose his house. What would he do with Tobias?

After the final note, Maggie stood. "Thank you, everyone. I'll see you after lunch." When they would practice Christmas carols to sing trapped on risers.

As the cast dispersed with their usual teasing and joking, Maggie returned to her seat. An apology to Mr. Anderson welled in her mouth, but she swallowed. An apology would be as unprofessional as begging for praise.

What should she do? She offered the thought as a prayer and felt a soft pressure to her throat, as if being silenced. As if being told to wait.

Mr. Anderson's eyes darted back and forth, and his mouth worked. On his far side, Ria caught Maggie's eye and gave her a prodding look.

Maggie raised a slight shrug. The man was thinking, and perhaps it was best not to interrupt. For good or ill.

"It's rough," he said.

For ill, but Maggie calmed her expression. "Yes, sir. We do have another three weeks."

His small gray eyes turned to her. “I like it.”

Ria’s brows shot high.

So did Maggie’s. But she injected confidence into her voice. “Thank you. We do too.”

The corners of his mustache turned down. “It needs work, mind you.”

A lot of work. “I know. We’ll practice hard.”

“I’ll write up some suggestions and bring them over in the morning.”

After he left the gym, Ria gripped Maggie’s arm. “Was he watching the same show we were?”

“I don’t know.” Had the Lord blinded him? “He’s a theater professional. Maybe he knows how a show tastes when it’s still half-baked.”

“Maybe. Anyway, I’m glad.”

“Me too. Thank you for all your help. I couldn’t do this without you.”

Ria made a scoffing sound. “Don’t you try to blame me for this mess.”

Maggie laughed, then sobered. “Please tell the cast the good news. I need to talk to Prescott.”

The cast was getting ready to leave for lunch. Off to himself, Prescott stashed props on the rack.

“Prescott? Are you all right?”

“Hmm?” His dull brown gaze turned to her. “Why do you ask?”

Maggie stepped closer and lowered her voice. “Your performance today was flat.”

He set Vi’s green hat on top of her green jerkin. “You want me out of the show.”

Not a question but a statement, and Maggie frowned. Why

would he think that? "No, I want you *in* the show. I don't know where you were today, but you weren't here."

In the background, a cheerful murmur rose to Ria's announcement.

Prescott's mouth mashed together, and pain flickered in his eyes. "I'm sorry. I ruined everything."

"No, you didn't. Mr. Anderson approved the show. But this afternoon, I need you here. All of you. Whatever's bothering you—leave it outside the gym."

The pain washed from his eyes, leaving something else behind, analyzing, pondering, determined. "You could have pandered to me as a star. Or because of my scars. You didn't. You were honest with me."

He'd probably received plenty of pandering, but what good would that do the show? "You're under the heel of a mean director, remember?" She did a cramp roll, which lost its zing without taps on her shoes.

He didn't laugh, and his expression shifted as if he were in a movie's climactic scene, shoving aside turmoil, rallying, resolving. "I'd like your opinion on something."

"What is it?"

"Saturday night. Are you free?"

"Yes."

"I'd like to take you to dinner at the Hotel del Coronado. You deserve an evening to celebrate. Then I'd like to ask your professional opinion."

Maggie's heart spiraled up into her throat. A romantic evening with Prescott? Or was it a business meeting?

Regardless, she'd get to dress up and go to the Del. "I'd love that."

CORONADO
SATURDAY, NOVEMBER 20, 1943

His order placed, Prescott thanked the waiter and returned his attention to Maggie, sitting partway around the round table facing the orchestra and dance floor.

Her loveliness strangled his breath. A long dress of sky blue brought out the color in her eyes and cheeks.

"This is so nice. Thank you again. I've always wanted to come here." She gave her head a little shake. "I must have said that a dozen times already."

He'd repeated himself a dozen times as well, his nervousness compounded by shame for his own cowardice. Taking her out "to celebrate"? Wanting her "professional opinion"?

Maggie had arched her eyebrows at his attaché case when he'd picked her up, but in the taxi and on the ferry, they'd had a comfortable conversation.

Now it was time, and he shifted on the cream cushion in his wicker chair. "I apologize for my performance the other day."

"You don't need—"

"I do. Something was bothering me, and that something is why I want your opinion."

Her lower lip poked out in confusion.

Prescott lifted his attaché case into his lap and opened it. "Do you remember the day you showed me the Old Globe and told me to write a new script for my life? Well, I did. It came out as an actual movie script." He set the stack of papers on the table.

"You did?" Her eyes and her voice lit in tandem. "That's wonderful."

"Don't get too excited." He latched his attaché case and set it by his chair. "I showed it to my agent on Tuesday. He said I'm not a writer."

"Oh no. How could he say such a thing?"

"He may be right."

"I'm so sorry. That was Tuesday? Then on Wednesday—the trial performance."

"It's no excuse. The first rule of this business is 'The show must go on.' I violated that rule—and when you needed me most."

"It all worked out." Her attention lay on the script alone. "Is this it? You brought it?"

His hand splayed on the papers as if protecting a child, but he rotated the stack in front of Maggie. "I'd like your honest opinion."

"Me? I'm not a writer. I never even acted in movies, only danced."

"You told me you fed yourself in Hollywood by typing scripts for the studio. I'm sure you can tell a good script from a bad one."

One corner of her red lips edged high. "I can."

"Tell me which one this is."

In her lap, Maggie twisted her hands together. She didn't want to disappoint him.

Prescott patted the script. "You can't hurt my feelings any more than Melvin did, and false praise won't do me any favors. Be honest."

"All right." Hesitancy stretched out her voice, but she stroked the top page. "You wrote this by hand?" She spoke not with disdain but with awe. "Is it difficult to write?"

One sharp nod. He wanted honesty, not sympathy.

He couldn't watch as Maggie started to read.

The circular ballroom spread before him, capped by the enormous red conical roof that could be seen from outside. Inside, tables and chairs ringed the dance floor, lit by crown-shaped lanterns and Moorish chandeliers.

As the orchestra played, couples swirled by, the men in blue naval officers' uniforms or black tuxedoes, the women in long gowns in every color imaginable.

How much courage would it take to ask Maggie to dance? Too much. She'd have to hold his disfigured hand. He was fooling himself even dreaming of romance.

A little gasp from Maggie, and she turned a page.

Prescott tried to read his own tortured handwriting from a bad angle. Where was she in the story?

He ripped his gaze away. Dancers eyed him as they passed. Did they recognize him from the movies? Pity his burns? Or were they confused by a couple sitting in silence as the lady read?

One song bled into another into another.

When the waiter brought their plates, Maggie looked up as if awakening. "Oh no. I have to stop reading, don't I?"

"If you'd like to eat," he said with a wry smile.

Maggie scooted the script to make room for her dinner. "I only have a few more pages. Poor Charles. He just lost his seat in Congress and the whole world hates him and he's alone at home. He wants a drink but plays the piano instead. And his warring emotions—anger, grief, shame, wanting to control his piano playing—failing. Every actor will want this role. In the right hands, he'll get an Oscar for sure."

Prescott closed his flopping mouth. "You think so?"

She narrowed one eye. "Why didn't your agent like it?"

"He just called it a mess. He only read one page though."

She shook her head a bit, making brown curls flutter. "I want to see this movie. I want to know what happens next. How much have you written?"

"The first act." He gestured to their plates. "We should eat."

A sheepish look, and she sliced her pork tenderloin. "I don't agree with Melvin. But I see why this was difficult. You've mentioned how much he means to you."

Prescott sliced his filet mignon into large bites to minimize the work. "He's like a second father."

"Your own father died when you were young, yes?"

Prescott stared at his utensils. He'd never told his whole story to anyone. Not Melvin. Not his friends. Not even the pastor at the rescue mission. But it needed to be told. Because it affected how he reacted to even a hint of rejection. Because it had affected Maggie.

He rubbed his thumb along the fork handle. "Pa died when I was twelve. I was big for my age, so I found work. Ma remarried a year later, but my stepfather—he hated me. Beat me. Said since I was working, why should he have to feed me? When I was fourteen, he kicked me out."

"Oh no." Maggie's voice quivered. "How could he do such a thing?"

The knife and fork pointed at each other. "Ma—she was standing in the doorway. I was out in the hall pleading with her. Where could I go? What could I do? But Ma—she feared him more than she loved me. She turned her back. Shut the door."

"Oh, Press." Maggie wiped her eyes with her handkerchief. What a horrible thing to endure. When Maggie was fourteen, her only concerns were passing Latin and getting the lead in the school play.

Prescott laid down his knife and fork. "When Melvin rejected my script, it felt like Ma's rejection all over again. I felt—worthless. It doesn't make sense, I know."

She leaned closer and resisted the urge to take his hand. "No, it does. And yet, it doesn't. Press, what she did to you—that was her fault, not yours. You mustn't ever see yourself as worthless. Ever."

His gaze flicked between Maggie and his plate, then a partial smile rose. "As Duke Orsino says, 'Thou knowst no less than all; I have unclasp'd to thee the book even of my secret soul.'"

Maggie's chest ached from the sweetness of the gift of the unclasping.

With a huff, Prescott picked up his fork and stabbed a green bean. "Once again, not an excuse for my poor performance, and I apologize."

Not an excuse, but an explanation—not only of his behavior, but of the story he'd written. "That's why your script is so strong. I feel what Charles is going through. The tragedies in your life—you've turned them into a story."

His brown-eyed gaze drifted up to her, wide with recognition. "That's what I want. I want to help people overcome. All those men in the hospital—they'll go home disfigured, disabled. They may lose their jobs, friends, sweethearts. I want my story to offer hope."

"It will. I know it will."

Light dawned in his expression, and it was glorious. "I can't tell you what it feels like to write. It's even better than acting.

As if this is what I was created for, what I was waiting for. As if everything in my life was leading to this."

Maggie's vision blurred, and she wiped her eyes again. "I'm so happy for you."

"I want to keep writing. I've had another couple of story ideas."

A sniffle, and Maggie dabbed her handkerchief at her nose. "You said your life was a blank page, but now look at you."

Prescott glanced around the ballroom. "Yeah, look at me, making a beautiful woman cry in public. Everyone thinks I'm breaking your heart."

One last dab, and Maggie stuffed her hankie in her handbag. "I won't have them thinking you're a bad egg. Let's dance." She set her hand on his.

He flinched.

She gasped and withdrew. "I'm sorry. Did that hurt?"

Prescott frowned at his fingers. "No. The scars are a bit tender, not painful. But you don't—you don't want to . . ."

She slid her hand over his, the taut pink skin, the ridges of scars, the bumps where fingers had once been. "I asked, didn't I?"

"You did." His voice rasped. He pushed back his chair, enveloped her hand in his, and led her past the railing and onto the sleek wooden floor.

Time to lighten the mood. "I always dreamed of dancing with Prescott Duke."

He chuckled and drew her into his arms. "You need better dreams, Maggie Oliver."

The warmth of him, the nearness of his face, the strength of his arms, the grace of his feet. Her breath—where had it gone? Somehow she managed a chuckle, managed to move her feet in a foxtrot as the orchestra played "Begin the Beguine."

Dancing with him was even better than she'd imagined. He led with considerate authority, with style and skill.

A smile rose from the joy of it. "I loved watching you dance in the studio and on the screen. The combination of manly athleticism and elegant grace."

"Which magazine did you read that in?"

She smiled at his teasing. But had she read it? Possibly. "Regardless, it's true."

Prescott twirled her past the stage. "Melvin said he discovered me because of my feet, how I moved in the ring. He also liked my looks, had me come in for a screen test."

His velvet voice would have sealed the deal. "Melvin spotted your talent."

Prescott's countenance darkened. "He says he didn't see talent in my script."

"Well, I did. So what will you do next? With the script?"

His thick tuxedo-clad shoulder lifted beneath her hand. "I don't know. I was hoping Melvin would pitch it."

"Is there anyone else you could talk to? Ask their opinion? You must know lots of people—producers, directors, studio heads."

"I do." His eyes darted as if cranked by the gears turning in his mind.

"First we need to type up your script."

Another shrug, paired with a grimace. "I don't have a typewriter, can't type."

"Silly goose." Maggie squeezed his shoulder. "I do and I can. Eighty words per minute."

"I can't ask you to—"

"You didn't ask. I volunteered." Her mouth rounded. "Tomorrow. Are you free? Are you attending a church in San Diego?

Come to ours. Grandpa would love to see you again. Sandwiches for lunch, then I'll type."

His feet slowed as anticipation battled with hesitancy on his face.

With gentle pressure on his shoulder, she urged him to resume the pace. "Please let me. I believe in this story, and I believe in you as a writer. If nothing else, you deserve your best shot at this dream."

All sorts of emotions warped his face.

Maggie laughed. "Oh no. Now everyone will think I'm making you cry. Dance."

With a self-conscious laugh, he spun her around, and her skirt fanned to the side.

Contentment settled inside. This might not be a romantic date, but neither was it a business meeting.

SEVEN

On the seventh day of Christmas my true love sent to me
. . . seven swans a-swimming.

SAN DIEGO
SUNDAY, NOVEMBER 21, 1943

"Maggie makes egg salad the same way Ethel did," Bill Curtis said.

"It's good." At the little kitchen table, Prescott took another bite of his sandwich and resisted the impulse to feed a morsel to the gray-and-white beggar beside his chair.

"Every Sunday, Ethel and I used to have egg salad and go to the zoo." Mr. Curtis separated a peeled orange and handed Prescott a fragrant slice. "The San Diego Zoo is one of the finest in the world."

"I've never been there." Prescott let the slice of California sunshine squirt in his mouth. He'd never been to any zoo. Yet another thing that didn't fit in the worlds of either poverty or glamour.

"It's still open. One of the few parts of Balboa Park unoccupied by the Navy." Sad longing clouded Mr. Curtis's eyes.

Maggie chuckled. "What would the Navy do with gorillas and hippos and flamingoes?"

Prescott smiled at the thought of a flamingo in a sailor hat. "If you miss it, Mr. Curtis, you should go."

His mouth pursed as if the orange had molded. "In my wheelchair? Never."

"I don't mind pushing," Maggie said.

Mr. Curtis hoisted himself up with one cane and took his plate to the sink. "I'm not making a fool of myself."

As Prescott chewed the last of his sandwich, the same pressure built as during his first USO hospital visit. "After my accident, I didn't go out in public unless necessary. I hate the stares. Worse, the pity."

"See, Maggie." Mr. Curtis ran water in the sink. "He understands."

"I do." Prescott stepped around Tobias and brought his plate to the sink, where Mr. Curtis took it. "I also understand it was killing me, avoiding all the things I loved."

"I get by." The man's voice came out gruff.

Prescott leaned back against the cabinet, so he could see both Maggie and her grandfather. "I know you do. So go to the zoo. I'll go with you. They'll be so busy gawking at me, they won't even notice you." He winked at Maggie.

She leaned her elbows on the table and grinned. "Can I go too?"

"Of course." He caught Mr. Curtis's eye. "All the men will be distracted by your granddaughter's beauty, and the women will be whispering to each other, 'Is that Prescott Duke? No, he was such a handsome fellow. Don't stare. It's rude.' No one will even notice you."

Maggie's smile wiggled.

Mr. Curtis harrumphed. "You two are ganging up on me."

"Of course," Maggie said. "What's the matter? You aren't chicken, are you?"

"Are you done with that?" Mr. Curtis took Maggie's plate without waiting for an answer. "It won't work. I can't take the wheelchair on the trolley."

Maggie gestured to the side. "It fits in your truck. You have a full tank of gas."

Mr. Curtis scrubbed at a plate with a rag. "I'm saving for an emergency. Gas is rationed, you know."

"Three gallons a week," Maggie said. "You haven't used three gallons in the past year."

Prescott shrugged. "Sounds like a lousy excuse to me."

"Fine." Mr. Curtis wiped the last plate under the faucet. "Next Sunday, then."

"No." Maggie raised one finger. "Not until Press finishes his script and I finish typing. It'll be our reward."

It was Prescott's turn to harrumph. "Now I'm being ganged up on."

"Absolutely. Get to work, young man." Maggie lifted a black typewriter case onto the kitchen table.

"Yes, ma'am." Prescott relished the familial teasing. But this wasn't his family.

Maggie sandwiched carbon paper between pieces of white paper and rolled the layers into her typewriter. "Have you decided where to pitch it?"

"I'll show it to Valentine Ruben." Prescott pulled his script out of his attaché case. "He's with my old studio and produced several of my films. The serious ones. We're pretty good friends. He visited a few times when I was in the hospital."

"This is a perfect fit for him." Maggie held out her hand for the script.

Prescott frowned at it. "This could be my swan song."

"You mustn't talk like that. This will be a glorious swan dive." She made a pretty swooping motion with one arm.

"'I forgive you the praise.'"

Maggie gave him a cute smile that said she recognized her Shakespearean cue. "'Alas, I took great pains to study it, and 't is poetical.'"

Once again, all Prescott wanted to do was to kiss her. But if he hadn't kissed her after dancing the night away at the Del, he certainly wouldn't do so in front of her grandfather.

Instead, he pulled a chair around beside her. "Can you decipher the first page?"

"This is where I'm stuck." Prescott stood, leaning his elbows on the chairback across from Maggie, his necktie and jacket long abandoned, his top buttons undone, his hair mussed. He'd never looked more attractive.

Maggie had just typed the scene where Charles Anthony despaired at the piano. "You don't know what Charles is going to do with his life?"

"No, I do. I do." Prescott pushed back from the chair, scooped up Tobias, and leaned against the wall near the window peeking into the living room. "Charles has money, he knows people with money and influence, and he's good at persuading people."

"A true politician."

Prescott rubbed Tobias behind his floppy ear. "Yes, but he used it all for his own power, at the expense of the woman and children he loved. Now he's going to use it to help women and children. He'll open a day care center, for free or cheap, for children of widows or women with disabled husbands. They need to work, but who's going to watch the kids?"

Maggie's fingers drifted from the keys to her lap. "I love the idea. Some of the factories provide day care now."

"Yes, but what about waitresses or salesgirls or maids? Who helps them? That's what Charles will do. He'll start it with his own money, recruit his pals to help. Charles won't take a penny himself. Not after the scandal."

"It's perfect. Why are you stuck?"

"How to get there." Prescott blew out a breath that ruffled Tobias's fur. "Her name is Laura Holt. She's a war widow, two little kids. She'll work for Charles, inspire him, challenge him."

"Fall in love with him?"

Prescott flicked up a smile. "If you're nice to me, I'll let them fall in love. But only near the end."

"His reward. Yes. This is going to be so good. How do they meet?"

"That's what I can't figure out." He walked toward the kitchen door. "I thought she was a waitress, but I want her to be unemployed. Or at church—but it lacks drama."

"A car accident?" Grandpa called from the living room.

Tobias wriggled, and Prescott set him down. Then Prescott's eyes widened, and he spun to the window. "You're a genius, Mr. Curtis."

"Finally, someone recognizes it."

"Hush, Grandpa." But Maggie loved that he was as caught up in the story as she was. "The real genius is at work."

Pacing, mussing his hair. He circled behind her chair, leaned over her shoulder, tapped the paper. "Exterior. Next day, late morning. City street."

Maggie's fingers went to work.

"Charles walks down the sidewalk, distracted, still in despair. He crosses a street against the light. Laura is driving a beat-up car, going too fast, children in the back. She turns. Charles doesn't see her. She swerves, hits a lamppost."

"Oh no." Keys clacked. "Is she hurt? Is he?"

"Charles dives out of the way, rolls, a few holes in his suit." Prescott's breath brushed Maggie's cheek. "He runs to the car. Her front end is smashed. She has a cut on her forehead. Charles presses a handkerchief to the cut. 'Are you hurt?'"

"She breaks down in tears."

"No!" Grandpa roared from the living room. "She's fierce, Maggie-mine. Fierce."

"Yes," Prescott said. "She has to be fierce to challenge Charles. But she's angry, scared. She swipes him away, checks on the kids. They tumbled to the floorboards, but they're okay."

"Oh, good." Maggie cleaned up Prescott's speech as she typed.

"She jumps out of the car, checks the front end, turns on Charles. 'Why don't you watch where you're going? Look at my car.'"

"Now she's late."

"Yes." Prescott clapped his hand to Maggie's shoulder. "Yes, now she's late. She's on her way to a job interview. That's how I'll connect it."

Maggie wanted to face him, but he was so close. "Why would she take her children to an interview?"

"Yeah, why? Why? She—she has no family—no one she trusts to babysit, anyway. She knows it'll hurt her chances in the interview, and she has no idea what to do with the kids if she gets the job. But what choice does she have? She needs the money."

Maggie poised her hands over the keys. "Ready?"

"No, let me think." He patted her shoulder, over and over, surely unaware he was touching her. "He'll offer to pay to fix her car. She'll turn him down."

"She doesn't want his charity. She wants a job."

"Yes. Charles argues she can't get a job without a car. Laura argues she can't get a job without a babysitter. Is he offering?"

"Oh, I like her. She's spunky. He offers her a job right then."

Prescott murmured. "Not yet. He hasn't come up with his idea. He'll talk her into taking the money, tell her to call if the cash doesn't cover the repairs, give her his card, take her number."

"There you go. You have your next scene, and it's a peach."

Prescott turned and grinned at her, so close she could touch his cheek and pull him in for a kiss.

If only.

With a dramatic flair, she set her fingers on the keys. "All right, Duke. Dictate away."

TUESDAY, NOVEMBER 30, 1943

Prescott and Vi finished act 1, scene 4, and they left the taped-off stage in the gymnasium.

In the other wing, Jack chatted with Albert, and Carol fussed with her fingernails.

"Scene 5," Maggie prompted.

Prescott tensed. Opening night was only ten days away, and too many players were still missing lines, cues, and marks.

"Carol, Jack," Maggie said. "Scene 5."

"Oh, sorry." Carol grabbed Jack and darted onto the stage.

Vi rolled her eyes at Prescott. She had memorized her lines long ago.

"Maggie!" Nan ran into the gymnasium with Ria on her heels, clutching at the red velvet dress hanging off one shoulder. "I can't possibly wear this. I'm swimming in it."

Indeed she was.

Nan stopped by Maggie's side and sobbed. "The costume girl won't listen to me."

Ria took Nan's arm in the full white sleeve. "Come back to the office. Maggie needs to work on the play."

The blonde's sobs only intensified.

"Hush, now." Maggie put her arm around Nan's shoulder and led her toward the door. "Everyone, take a short break. And practice your lines. Come along, Nan."

"Poor Maggie," Vi muttered. "She has enough theatrics onstage."

"She does." But she'd handled Nan's scene with grace.

"I wish everyone knew their parts." Her voice low, Vi tipped her head toward Carol—who was not practicing. "You do."

Prescott settled into a chair in the "wings" of the stage. "Honestly, Duke Orsino is one of the easier roles. I only have four scenes. You have a heavy load, but you're doing great."

"Viola is such fun to play." Vi took a seat beside him, her hair and eyes shining.

Yet her talent outshone her looks. "Did you ever do a screen test for a speaking role?"

She crinkled her nose. "A few offers. For a price I refused to pay."

Prescott groaned. "I'm sorry you ladies are subjected to that. It's wrong."

"That's why I like the USO. All of the fun, none of the funny business."

On the far side of the gym, Greta practiced her acrobat routine with five big gold rings.

"I could probably get you a legitimate screen test," Prescott said.

Vi shook her head hard, blonde hair swinging.

"I could come along, make sure everyone behaves."

"It's sweet of you, but I'm not interested."

Prescott blinked at her. "You're not?"

"Sure, it was fun dancing in musicals, and the USO is a hoot. But this isn't what I want for my life."

"What do you want?"

Vi glanced toward the door. "Don't tell Maggie. I don't want her to worry about me being distracted. But I was accepted into nursing school. I start in January."

Prescott had lost his Hollywood dream, and Vi had set hers aside. Chosen a new path. So had Prescott. "I'm happy for you. And I won't tell Maggie."

Vi reached over and squeezed his knee. "Thanks for the offer—and for understanding."

He winked at her. "Knock 'em dead, kid."

"I certainly hope not." Vi recoiled in mock horror. "Nurses are supposed to save lives, not take them."

They laughed together.

"Oh, Maggie's back," Vi said. "Nan all straightened out?"

"For now." Maggie stopped about ten feet away with a strained smile. A glance at Prescott's knee—and Vi's hand—and the smile vibrated. "Let's get back to work, everyone. Scene 5."

Vi left her seat to chat with Barbara.

But Prescott sat still with a funny feeling in his gut. Was Maggie jealous? Of him and Vi? A surge of pleasure. Could she be interested in him romantically? Some men would play up the jealousy, but Prescott hated games. And he liked Maggie. A lot.

The fifth scene progressed. Faltered. It contained lots of witty banter and entrances and exits. Many of the actors missed cues. Carol, playing Maria, didn't know her lines.

"Carol, do you hear the cadence?" A thread of frustration wound through Maggie's usual patience. "How the jester's lines flow into yours, flow out of yours?"

Carol's shoulders slumped. "It's too hard. Too many lines. I'm used to doing comedy bits, not Shakespeare."

"I'd like to see you spending more time reading your script and less time chatting with your friends." Maggie's words carried both gentleness and a backbone.

Prescott tapped his fingers on his knees. Carol had been singing with Prescott three times a week in the hospital—when she could have been studying her lines.

"Carol, you're perfect for Maria," Maggie said. "You bring zest and humor to this role. I know you can do it."

If only Prescott could put his arm around Maggie's shoulder as she'd done for Nan. She hadn't flinched from his touch when she was typing.

A small smile rose. They'd spent two Sundays in a row at her house, plus the Friday after Thanksgiving, typing and bouncing ideas off each other while Mr. Curtis followed along.

He was determined to finish his script before opening night. After that, meeting to type would grow difficult.

Yet all he wanted was to slow down the process so he could savor it.

"Pause right there." Despite the panic in Maggie's chest, she aimed a calm expression at the five comedic players. "Freddie, Sir Toby is the key to this scene. He teases Sir Andrew, banters with Maria and the jester, and taunts Malvolio. His clever use of words is vital. You must slow down."

Freddie waved her off. "Sir Toby is quick-witted. He talks fast."

"But onstage, you must slow down, especially with Elizabethan speech. If the audience doesn't understand Sir Toby's line, they won't understand Sir Andrew's misunderstanding of that line."

Freddie's eyelids fluttered as if he wanted to roll his eyes.

"Slow down. Enunciate. Start over." Maggie returned to her seat. After four days off for Thanksgiving, the cast had fallen behind, and she had so little time before opening night.

"Miss Oliver!" Mrs. Laverne stomped across the gym, her face bright red, her arms swinging hard.

"Just a minute, please." Maggie held up one hand to the club director so the scene onstage could play out.

Mrs. Laverne stepped right in front of her chair and glared down at her. "Mrs. Buffington saw one of your girls swanning around the club half-dressed."

Maggie sighed, rose, and glanced over Mrs. Laverne's shoulder at the actors. "Take a short break. Study your lines."

Now Mrs. Laverne glared up at her. "I will not stand for this."

With difficulty, Maggie assumed her most soothing expression. "I do apologize. The lady was having a costume fitting in my office, and—"

"Lady? Ladies don't parade in front of gentlemen with their clothes falling off."

Ria jogged into the gym. "I'm sorry, Miss Oliver. I was explaining to Mrs. Laverne—"

"Some things don't need explaining." Mrs. Laverne wheeled on Ria.

Ria didn't back down. "I told the actress to stay in the office."

"And I escorted her back immediately," Maggie said. "Other than one bared shoulder, I assure you everything was proper."

"Nothing proper about Hollywood floozies—"

"I beg your pardon." Maggie's chest stiffened, and so did her tone. "These ladies passed the same screening as your volunteers, took the same training. They signed contracts promising to behave in a manner consistent with public decency and morality. Please do not insult them."

"I'm calling Mr. Anderson." Mrs. Laverne stomped away.

Ria gripped Maggie's arm. "I'll call him first. I run faster than she does." Indeed, Ria passed Mrs. Laverne before she reached the door.

"Go, Ria. Go," Maggie muttered, and she rubbed her forehead.

Prescott stood close to Vi, talking low, and an ugly pang added to the throbbing in Maggie's head. After so many pleasant days typing together, she'd thought something special was developing between them. Apparently, she was mistaken.

And apparently, quite selfish. If she truly cared about Prescott, she'd want him to be happy, even with Vi.

But was it wrong to want happiness for herself? And for Frank?

Prescott and Vi came up to Maggie, and Vi laid her hand on Maggie's arm. "We're sorry this is happening. Is there any way we can help?"

They were such good friends, and she gave a rueful smile. "Help Carol learn her lines?"

Vi glanced away. "I'll talk to her right now."

"Thank you."

After Vi left, Prescott stepped closer. "I'm praying for you. That's the best help."

"It is. Thanks." Maggie rubbed circles on her temple. She'd been so busy, she hadn't sat down with her prayer notebook for days. And listening took even more time than listing.

"About Carol," Prescott said with his smooth voice. "She sings for the hospital shows. She's excellent, but she could use that time to study. What if Vi took her place?"

Maggie's throat closed off. A nurse served as Prescott's liaison within the hospital, but Frank escorted the singers to the hospital.

"I told Frank about Vi's star quality. She'd be a huge hit with the fellows." Warmth filled Prescott's brown eyes. "He thinks it's meant to be. The street he grew up on was called Violet Lane."

So that was where Vi got her stage name. How utterly romantic! And how utterly unromantic to meet again at the park gate. And with opening night only a week and a half away.

"Maggie?" Prescott said with a frown.

She raised a smile that felt fake. "It's a great idea, but Vi has the largest female part in the show."

"Too much, huh?"

"I'll ask another girl to take Carol's place. I'll do it myself if necessary."

"I wouldn't mind." Prescott winked at her.

Maggie managed to smile despite the twisting in her stomach. Now she was officially meddling.

EIGHT

On the eighth day of Christmas my true love sent to me . . .
eight maids a-milking.

SUNDAY, DECEMBER 5, 1943

It was one thing to read about the immensity of elephants and giraffes and hippos, and another to actually see it.

Prescott leaned on the rail, squeezed beside Maggie and Mr. Curtis. A male hippo named Rube, according to the sign, lounged at one end of the pool, with only his eyes and ears poking above the surface. Closer to the rail, his mate, Ruby, lay on her side underwater while her baby nursed.

Maggie's hair concealed her cheeks as she leaned over. "I've never thought of hippos nursing before."

Her grandfather gave her a teasing grin. "They *are* mammals."

"But underwater—that's incredible."

Prescott pointed. "Here comes the baby."

The little hippo pushed to the surface, gulped a breath of air, and dove for more milk—while dozens of visitors gasped and cooed.

The moment Prescott saw the article in the *San Diego Union* last week about the baby's debut, he knew he could overcome Mr. Curtis's remaining objections to the trip.

Maggie held back her hair to smile at Prescott. "This is worth staying up late tonight to type, isn't it?"

"It is. Only ten pages left anyway."

"The ending." She nudged him. "Can't wait."

"Let's let these youngsters have a look." Mr. Curtis hobbled back to his wheelchair, and a pair of little girls rushed into the gap.

Prescott pushed the chair, following Maggie, who carried the map. She'd padded the wheelchair handles with fabric for him, which helped. But he wouldn't have minded bare metal if it meant spending a day with these two.

Maggie dashed to the next enclosure. "Aren't you the funniest-looking creature?"

Prescott heaved a pretend sigh. "That's not a nice way to talk about me."

She laughed and pointed to a large pig-shaped animal with a floppy snout, like a shorter version of an elephant's trunk. "It's a tapir, the sign says."

"That's Trudy." Mr. Curtis accepted Prescott's help in standing. "She's an escape artist. She got out about two years ago. They found her in a storm drain."

Prescott wiggled his nose like a tapir until Maggie laughed.

A sky as gray as the elephants in the pen behind him promised rain soon, but he didn't care with Maggie beside him.

How he would miss their Sundays together—church, lunch, typing, talking.

After opening night on Friday, they'd have a flurry of performances through Christmas Eve. Then . . . nothing.

Maggie opened the colorful illustrated map. "We'll go up 'F' Canyon to see the bears and seals and polar bears and lions. Then down 'G' Canyon to see the lesser pandas—oh, they're new—and the cats and wolves and camels and kangaroos."

Prescott bore Mr. Curtis's weight as the man eased down into the wheelchair. "We'll finish before dark?"

"Nowhere near." Mr. Curtis settled into his seat. "This is a huge zoo."

"We'll come back another day." Maggie folded the map. "I know. To celebrate when Press sells his script."

Prescott's shoulders tensed, but he was committed. He was having lunch with Valentine Ruben on Tuesday when Maggie was holding rehearsals for the ladies.

"Mr. Ruben will love it." Maggie led the way past the giraffes they'd already admired. "The story is wonderful. Oscars all around."

Prescott pushed the wheelchair down the path. "Too bad they don't give Oscars for best performance at a Smith-Corona."

She tossed him a little smile over her shoulder. "Just put me in the credits."

"You're getting ahead of yourself."

"Not at all. You've done the hard work of writing the screenplay and the courageous work of scheduling that meeting."

Prescott shrugged. Courage? A courageous man wouldn't choose the zoo for a date with the woman he loved. And he did love her. No doubt remained.

They rounded the corner by the canteen. An older couple eyed his scars in passing, and Prescott gave them a smiling nod. His scars didn't feel ugly now that he realized they connected him with others who were scarred, outside or inside. The scars might even be a gift.

"Oh no, Grandpa! Bears." Maggie crouched on the far side of the wheelchair.

Mr. Curtis glanced back at Prescott. "Nothing in the world scared Maggie-mine when she was little. Except bears."

"Save me, Grandpa." A giggle bubbled up.

How good to see Maggie's natural enthusiasm returning after a trying week of rehearsals.

Mr. Curtis snorted. "Asking an old man in a wheelchair? Nah. I retired. You've got a big strapping man here. Let him help you."

Mischief frolicked in Maggie's blue eyes as she peeked up at him. "Save me, Press."

Nothing he wanted more than to pull her into his arms. Yet . . . something else felt more appropriate. "Sorry, kid. I'm a city boy. You're on your own."

"Press!" She sprang to her feet, laughed, and swatted him lightly in the chest.

"Say, Mr. Curtis," he said. "I think I need saving from her."

"I liked you better when you weren't saucy," she said. "No—not true. This is better."

It was indeed better, and he returned her grin full force. Now that he had an aim in life, he intended to pursue her.

Maggie found a spot at the railing around the kangaroo enclosure while Prescott helped Grandpa to standing.

All afternoon, Prescott had assisted Grandpa with respectful regard, never patronizing. Because he understood. What a thrill to watch the change in him, opening, relaxing, gaining in purpose.

Sweet tenderness nestled in her chest. This was more than a crush on a movie star. This felt like love. And not once all day had he mentioned Vi.

Before her, kangaroos rested in the cool gray afternoon or nibbled on the grass.

A couple rolled a stroller to the rail beside Maggie, and the parents chatted with three older children about the kangaroos. In the stroller sat a baby around one year old with a ruffled bonnet over a cap of dark blonde hair. Her little face reddened and wrinkled, and she dropped her bottle in her lap. It rolled down over pudgy pink legs.

"Oh no." Maggie grabbed the glass bottle and handed it to the mother. "Excuse me, ma'am. Your baby dropped her bottle. I didn't want it to break and spill all her milk."

"Thank you so much," the mother said. "What if the nipple tore? It's hard to buy anything made of rubber with the war on."

The mother returned to explaining to her other children that a group of kangaroos was called a mob, but the baby squirmed. Soon she'd squall and put an end to the family's excursion.

Not if Maggie could help it. She knelt beside the stroller and put on the happy voice that never failed her with children. "Hello. Do you see the kangaroos? Aren't they funny?"

The redness dissipated in the baby's face, and she sat forward. "Da."

"That's right. Kan-ga-roos. See the kangaroos go hop, hop, hop?" Maggie curled her hands in front of her chest like a kangaroo, and she bounced her shoulders. "Hop, hop, hop."

A smile dipped into the little round cheek.

"Hop, hop, hop." Maggie made her voice bounce. "Hop, hop, hop."

A wet little giggle erupted.

"Takes me back," Grandpa said.

Leaning on the railing, he and Prescott smiled down at her.

"You entertaining your brother and sister," Grandpa said. "Boy, could you make them laugh."

Maggie resumed her hop, hop, hopping. Rose would especially love it.

Now the baby's brothers hopped like kangaroos, and baby giggles turned to full-blown laughter.

The mother gave Maggie a grateful look and pushed the stroller after her mob of little kangaroos.

"So you started your career in entertainment at a young age." Prescott offered her a hand.

"I did." Maggie accepted the warm gift and relinquished it reluctantly after she stood. "I loved making Rose smile."

In fact, she'd loved it too much.

Her cheek twitched.

When Maggie came home sick from first grade, Mama had ordered her to stay away from Rose. But little Rose had begged at Maggie's door. How could she resist?

Maggie shoved away from the rail and forced a smile. "Shall we find the zebras?"

"Not if you want to do any typing tonight." Grandpa limped to his wheelchair. "Sun's getting low."

It was. The dimness of the sky matched the strange dimness in her heart.

HOLLYWOOD
TUESDAY, DECEMBER 7, 1943

Prescott hadn't eaten at the Hollywood Brown Derby for two years. At a booth in the back sat Valentine Ruben.

The acclaimed producer stood and pumped Prescott's hand. "Good to see you, Press."

"Good to see you too, Val." The man would blow away in a stiff wind, but he carried great weight in Hollywood. "How are Stella and the kids?"

Val motioned to the tufted leather booth, and the men sat beneath dozens of framed caricatures. On the far side of the restaurant, Prescott's caricature hung on the wall.

"The twins are in their sophomore year of college." Val picked up his menu. "One at USC, one at UCLA. You can imagine what it's like when both girls come home."

Prescott laughed. "And Stella?"

"Wonderful as ever." Small dark eyes shone. "What are you up to lately? I haven't heard from you in—what?—over a year?"

"At least that long." Prescott didn't want to talk business before ordering lunch. He planned to have the Brown Derby's signature Cobb salad, but with his stomach flopping around, how could he eat? He picked up the menu. Set it down. "Until recently, I haven't been up to anything. It's been killing me."

Val's broad forehead warped. "I can't imagine what I'd do . . ."

If he lost his career? But a genuine smile rose. "Right now I'm in a USO show in San Diego, and it's a peach."

"That's swell. I'm glad to hear it."

After the waiter took their orders, Val leaned skinny arms on the table. "I was a little surprised when you called out of the blue."

Val knew something was up. Prescott shot up a quick prayer and remembered a fortifying speech by Olivia in *Twelfth Night*: *"Alas, it is the baseness of thy fear that makes thee strangle thy propriety; Fear not, Cesario, take thy fortunes up."*

For too long, fears had strangled Prescott. No longer. "I wanted to discuss something with you—a script."

"A script?" Val cocked his head of tight black curls. "Melvin found a role for—"

"I wrote the script."

Val's eyebrows arched high, then drooped low.

"I know," Prescott said. "Mel always says actors shouldn't write. In all honesty, I showed the script to Mel. He only read one page, but he didn't like it."

Val sagged back in his seat. "Why even mention it to me?"

"I—I'm not trying to go over Melvin's head. He's been my agent as a performer, and I'd want him to be my agent as a writer. I just—I wanted another opinion before I followed his advice and gave up."

Val's thin chest expanded. "Mel has a good eye for scripts. One of the many reasons I like working with him and his talent."

Prescott managed to crack a smile. "I'm no good at pitching, am I?"

"No, you're not." But Val mirrored his smile.

Too much heart and courage and effort had gone into the story to stop now. He opened his attaché case and pulled out over a hundred pages covered in Maggie's neat typing, not a crossed-out word in sight. He could still see her pretty face as she proclaimed, "Oscars all around." Perhaps he should have had Maggie do the pitching.

"I believe in this story." Prescott held it tight. "It's about a man who has everything, loses everything, and makes a new and better life."

Val didn't look at the pages, only at Prescott. "Listen, I'm sorry all this happened to you. I loved working with you. Not just because you're talented, but because you knew when to take direction and when to stick to your guns. And you never let fame go to your head. You treated everyone on set well, from the director to the janitor."

Prescott shrugged. "My mother was a maid."

"I also know you didn't get far in school. I'm sorry, Press. I wish I could help, but . . ."

Prescott should stash away his work, collect himself, and enjoy lunch with his friend. But there on the page, Charles Anthony's name stared up at him.

"All that happened to me . . ." Prescott's voice rasped, and he cleared his throat. "These scars—this is why I'm the right person to tell this story. Men are coming home from the war disfigured, broken. They've seen horrible things. Some of them have done horrible things. This story—it's powerful, Val."

Something melted in Val's expression, but not enough.

A great wave of frustration swelled inside, and he set the script in front of Val. "Listen, why don't you take it home? Read five, ten pages. If you hate it, that'll be the end of it. I'll never bother you with a script again."

Studying him, Val shifted his lower jaw from side to side. He groaned and drew the script closer. "Don't tell anyone I'm getting soft in my old age."

"Not a soul. And thanks." It was over. He felt it. But he'd done his best.

SAN DIEGO
THURSDAY, DECEMBER 9, 1943

Sitting in the Old Globe during the dress rehearsal, Maggie kept holding her breath—and releasing it in wondrous relief.

For the final number, Prescott stood center stage. The green velvet jerkin accentuated his broad shoulders and solid torso and set off his dark hair and eyes. He finished his final emcee bit, charming and generous, and sang, "'On the twelfth day of Christmas my true love sent to me—twelve drummers drumming . . .'"

The band's drummer broke into a jazzy solo while the cast of *Twelfth Night* ran onto the stage for their bows. The jester tripped the villain Malvolio, milking one last laugh.

"'Eleven pipers piping . . .'" The band stood and held instruments high.

"'Ten lords a-leaping . . .'" The men bounded out for their bows.

"'Nine ladies dancing . . .'" They twirled onto the stage, their red velvet skirts floating even more beautifully than Maggie had imagined.

Each act came in turn, no bumping, no missed cues, down to Vi's partridge curtsy with a hand over her heart. Then the whole cast, in alternating red and green, sang "Happy Holiday."

Maggie bolted to her feet and applauded. "That was perfect. I'm so proud of all of you."

"I thought a good dress rehearsal was bad luck," Freddie called.

"Don't worry," Ferdy said. "We'll botch up the next run-through for good measure."

"Don't you dare," Maggie said with a laugh. "Twenty-minute break, one last run-through, then the cast party at the U.S.

Grant Hotel tonight. A huge thank you to Prescott for hosting us."

The cast cheered and whistled.

When they retreated backstage, Maggie stretched her shoulders, but her mind whirled.

"Hi there." Prescott sat on the edge of the stage, smiling in an inquiring way, as if he sensed her jumbled thoughts. "What do you think?"

Maggie's breath flowed out, and she plopped into her seat. "It went well."

"I agree." He hopped to the floor and took a seat beside her. "And yet . . . ?"

"And yet, Freddie's right. Every theater person knows a bad dress rehearsal means a good opening night. And vice versa."

Prescott leaned his elbow on the armrest between them. "You believe in superstition?"

"No, but—"

"No buts." He gave her a firm look. "I know you have a lot at stake. Your job, your grandpa's home."

Maggie twisted her hands together on top of her portfolio. "All the bigwigs will be here tomorrow—city leaders and admirals and Mr. Anderson and other head honchos in the USO. Even Grandpa."

"The biggest wig of all." Prescott leaned closer. "Remember, half the problems we see onstage will be invisible to the audience. They won't know if Carol skips a line and Albert covers for her. And other problems—well, they're good for laughs, and we're here to make the boys laugh."

"We are." Her fingers fell still.

Prescott put his hand on hers, and his warmth and calm seeped through to her. "You've done excellent work. This show will be every bit the spectacle you dreamed of."

For almost two months, Maggie had encouraged Prescott. With success. He'd given his script to the producer, and Val had promised to call in a week or so. Now Prescott was encouraging her. As if she weren't already hopelessly in love. She swallowed hard. "Thank you."

He squeezed her hand. "I need to visit the water cooler before the others drain it dry." He leaned forward, his mouth rounded as if to give her a kiss—the quick and easy kiss of a couple completely comfortable with each other.

He stopped. His eyes went wide. He retracted his lips, patted her hand, and marched backstage.

Maggie's breath whooshed out. Had he meant to kiss her? His screen kisses sent her into palpitations. But to receive one? Not a screen kiss but a real one. Could her heart stand it?

"Miss Oliver?" Frank Sebastian strode down the aisle, waving with a broad grin. "How's the rehearsal going?"

The stage was empty, but not for long. Maggie darted up the aisle, took Frank's arm, and steered him back toward the lobby. "It's going well, but not if the cast sees you here."

"What do you mean?" Frank struggled to keep up.

"Show people are superstitious." Maggie shoved open the lobby door and closed it in blessed concealment. "They consider it bad luck if someone watches a dress rehearsal."

Frank frowned at the door. "I'd like to see the show."

"After the opening night craziness is over, you can come to any performance you'd like. However, tomorrow evening at the end of the show, I do have a special treat for you to thank you."

His face blanched. "I don't need—"

"I insist. Come to the lobby at nine o'clock sharp. Ria will meet you and let you in when it's time—and not before." Even Ria had no inkling about Maggie's surprise.

"You're not bringing me onstage, are you?" He turned a bit green, and he laid a hand on his stomach. "I've got horrible stage fright. Get real jittery. My stomach . . ."

He wouldn't throw up, would he? Maggie kept her smile high. "I promise, you'll love this treat."

All his jitters would flee the moment he saw his beloved Vernice.

NINE

On the ninth day of Christmas my true love sent to me . . .
nine ladies dancing.

THURSDAY, DECEMBER 9, 1943

After dinner, Prescott rose to address the cast members, all formally dressed and seated at banquet tables at the U.S. Grant Hotel.

He'd thrown the party to celebrate what they'd accomplished and to give the cast one last chance to have fun together. After opening night, they'd have three shows a day through Christmas Eve, with only Wednesdays off.

"Here's to all of you, for a job well done." Prescott turned to Ria, seated to his left. "And to Ria Fernandez, the brains and hands behind this operation."

Everyone applauded Ria, with a few well-deserved whistles, and Ria flapped her hand to stop them.

Prescott faced Maggie to his right. "And to Maggie, who had the imagination to envision this show, the determination to make it come to pass, and the heart to bring us all together."

More cheers and whistles, and Maggie ducked her chin modestly.

"Now you may open your Christmas gifts." He gestured to the boxes at each place and took his seat. He'd had the jeweler's shop wrap the ladies' gifts in red and the men's in green.

Paper ripped, and pleased murmurs circled the room as the men inspected cuff links engraved with the numeral "12" and the ladies donned bracelets with charms for each of the twelve days of Christmas.

"Oh, Press, it's perfect." Maggie twisted her wrist, making charms jangle.

"This show—these people—they've meant a lot to me." His voice roughened. Maggie meant the most.

"Come on, kids." Freddie sprang to the piano. "This is supposed to be a party."

A lively tune spilled out, and jitterbugs sprang up and filled the little dance floor.

Maggie leaned closer. "I'm surprised they aren't tired of dancing by now."

"Come on, Press." Greta grabbed his arm. "I never got to dance with you. Vi's been hogging you."

Prescott stumbled after the redhead, laughing, and he shrugged at Maggie, who laughed right back at him.

He wasn't much of a jitterbug, but he could swing, and Greta's pretty face lit up as they danced.

Wearing a long red dress, Maggie twirled around the floor with Albert. Prescott caught her eye and grinned at her. She was responsible for the show's success, and she was the one he wanted to dance with.

But when the song ended, Nan cut in. Then Carol. In the next hour, he'd danced with all nine ladies in the cast. Twice.

He kept glancing at Maggie and making her laugh with exaggerated exhausted expressions.

Not once did she act as she had when Vi had her hand on his knee. Not even when he danced with Vi. Either he was mistaken and she wasn't interested, or she was interested but not the jealous sort.

Tonight he was determined to find out. He might not ever become a screenwriter, but he'd find work. He'd made inquiries, and the situation wasn't as hopeless as he'd thought. The type of work didn't matter, as long as it was honest and helped people.

The song ended, and Barbara heaved a sigh, her cheeks red from exertion. "I'm worn out. Hey, Nan, you ready to call it a night?"

All around, cast members picked up purses and gift boxes.

Prescott hadn't danced with Maggie yet. And where had she gone?

The door leading outside stood open, and a long red skirt passed through. Maggie's.

A fortifying breath. It was time.

Finally, a break in the rain. Maggie strolled out into the Palm Court on the roof of the hotel's ground floor, surrounded by the three wings of the eleven-story hotel, its windows darkened for the blackout. Potted palms and an ornate fountain adorned the court, and muted moonlight glimmered on the rain-dampened pavement.

She'd always wanted to see the Palm Court. Standing in Horton Plaza across Broadway, she could only catch glimpses of the elegance.

"You never gave me a chance to dance with you." Prescott's voice flowed from behind her, as velvety as the night sky.

He'd followed her? Now the evening was perfect.

Prescott sauntered closer, so manly and suave in his tuxedo, like a scene in a movie.

That was her cue, and she gave him a playful smile. "I already danced with you."

Still closer he came. "Not tonight."

She clasped her hands behind her back. "The song says, 'Nine ladies dancing,' and you already danced with nine. I wouldn't want to ruin it."

"What if I dream of dancing with Maggie Oliver?" Under the teasing tone lay a whisper of wistfulness.

How could she resist? She took his outstretched hand. "You need better dreams, Prescott Duke."

He pulled her close, and his chuckle tickled her temple. Freddie had stopped playing the piano, but she rocked in romantic silence in Prescott's sturdy arms. Maggie inhaled the scent of him, the warmth of him.

Prescott drew in a deep breath. "I'm surprised Frank Sebastian isn't here."

Maggie dipped her chin. She would have invited Frank if the party landed just one day later. "Only Ria and I know him, and not very well."

"Oh? I . . . thought you might be sweet on him."

Maggie pulled back to look him in the eye. He was serious? "On Frank? Goodness, no. He's just a kid."

"All right." He pulled her close again to dance.

She resisted. She wasn't going to let him off the hook so easily. "Why do you ask?" She kept her tone light, although her heart galloped.

Prescott rearranged his hand on her waist. His gaze darted

to the side and back again. "You were honest with me about my script, and now I'm asking for an honest answer. Do I stand a chance with you?"

She swayed a bit closer. "You aren't sweet on Vi?"

"On Vi? She's just a kid too. No, it's you. It's always been you. Be honest. Do I stand a chance?" His gaze plumbed the depths of hers. Such pain, such longing, such vulnerability.

"Oh, Press." Even in the most dramatic of her dreams, she'd never imagined this scene.

"Please," he said. "I'm falling in love with you, but if you aren't interested, say the word. I'll never speak of it again."

Maggie released his hand, and she caressed his cheek, his beautiful scarred cheek. "I had a horrible crush on you on the silver screen. But in person—oh, Press, you've stolen my heart completely."

He enveloped her in his arms, in his kiss, and he groaned.

Maggie gasped and pulled away. "Oh no. Did that hurt?"

"Come back here," he said in a husky voice.

She did as he asked.

If she were in a movie, she would have instructed her legs to go limp and her torso to melt into his, but her body needed no such direction. Only his strong embrace kept her standing. And her heart—the palpitations!

Prescott burrowed in her neck. "Oh, Maggie. 'If it be thus to dream, still let me sleep!'"

She smiled over the broad expanse of his shoulders. Sebastian's line to Olivia and entirely appropriate. "I don't want to awaken either."

He chuckled. "Since Frank and Vi aren't spoken for, perhaps we should introduce them. Let those two kids find love as well."

Bubbles frolicked in her chest. "Want to hear a little secret? They're already in love."

Prescott's chin drew back. "They're dating?"

"They dated in high school. They were engaged."

He tipped his head to the side. "I thought her fiancé was lost at sea."

"That was Frank." She rose on her toes to get closer. "By the time the news got home that he was alive, Vi had run away to Hollywood and changed her name from Vernice Lingenfelter to Violet Lane. Frank hasn't been able to find her."

"Violet Lane . . . That was the street—"

"Isn't it romantic? And tomorrow night, they'll be reunited."

"Tomorrow?"

"After the curtain call." Maggie settled her heels back to earth, and she played with the lapels of Prescott's tux. "Frank will be waiting in the lobby—I told him I had a surprise for him. Ria will let him in when I give the signal. Ria doesn't know why. It's my surprise. And yours now too." She reached up to kiss him.

He leaned back. "In front of an audience?"

"Won't it be romantic? They'll see each other. She'll cry. He'll run to comfort her. They'll meet partway and—"

"If—if it were Hollywood."

Why wasn't he smiling? "What do you mean?"

"Maggie . . ." Prescott released her and stepped back, his hands low on his hips, his chin tucked to his chest. "In real life, people don't act like they do in Hollywood. Or in Shakespeare."

Maggie's empty hands fluttered together, chilled. "I—I don't understand."

He waved one arm to the side. "In *Twelfth Night*, when Duke

Orsino finds out Cesario is actually Viola, he instantly falls in love. In real life, he'd have some questions for her. Might even be angry that she'd deceived him."

Maggie's shoulders squirmed. "It's a comedy."

"Yes, but Frank and Vi's story—it's not a comedy. It's a tragedy. Vi thinks Frank is dead. Dead, Maggie. She'll be shocked."

"Yes, but then she'll—"

"How do you know?" Prescott's voice grew in intensity, in severity. "People in shock—you never know how they'll act."

"It'll be fine." Maggie hugged herself and glanced away from that unwarranted severity. "They'll be thrilled to see each other."

"What if they aren't? What if they don't act the way you've imagined? It's in public. In front of a crowd. This sort of thing should be a private matter, not in the limelight."

Maggie winced. True, some people didn't like a fuss—for reasons she couldn't begin to fathom. But the vision for Frank and Vi wouldn't leave her mind. "Don't you see how beautiful it will be?"

"Beautiful?" Prescott's tone dove deep and dark. "For you or for them?"

She gasped. "Pardon?"

"This isn't entertainment." His voice and his gaze sliced. "These are real lives, real hearts, broken hearts. Not actors on your stage to be directed."

How could he say such things about her? Maggie's fingers dug into her own arms. "That's not what I think. Frank and Vi are my friends. I care about them. I'm helping them. After all their years of unhappiness, they deserve this. It's a Christmas gift."

Prescott's face warped, and he rubbed the back of his neck. "If you truly cared for them, you'd tell them in private. In fact, you would have already done so."

A twinge of pain. She did feel bad about the delay, but that was a moot point now anyway. "It—it'll be fine. I know it."

"Always so sure of yourself. You can be wrong, you know."

"I know that." Her voice warbled, and she swallowed hard. "But this—this feels right."

He stared down toward Maggie's shoes. His jaw ground in circles. "I can't love a woman who cares more for spectacle than she does for people. I can't."

She refused to raise her voice, refused to cry or make a scene. "So that's it? It's over?"

With his gaze still fixed on her shoes, he gave one sharp nod.

One thing Hollywood had taught her was how to make a graceful exit, so she kept her chin high, crossed the court, and opened the door to the reception room.

The charms on the bracelet flashed gold in the lamplight.

Twelve days of Christmas . . .

Oh no. The show.

Not only had she lost the man she loved, but she'd also lost her star.

To think he'd thought he was in love with her.

Maggie paused with her hand on the doorknob, then she darted inside.

Another door slammed in Prescott's face, and he winced and pressed his hands over his eyes.

She didn't love him enough to listen to him. Maggie was just like Ma, choosing her own path heedless of other people. Could Maggie's scheme work as she imagined? For Frank and Vi's sakes, he prayed it would. But if it failed . . .

Maybe he could find Vi and warn her.

Prescott trudged back to the reception room, empty of all but dirty dishes, rumpled napkins, and shreds of wrapping paper.

Grief ballooned inside. Only half an hour earlier, this room had overflowed with laughter, celebration, the hope of love.

He slapped a hand to the table for balance. Red paper. Green paper. Opening night.

How could he pull himself together enough to play the emcee and act and dance and sing? And why should he? For her?

Prescott crumpled some paper.

What would happen to the show if he didn't perform?

Disaster. And disaster would serve her right.

He groaned and bowed over the table. How petty could he get? What about the men in the audience who came to be entertained? What about the cast who'd poured their hearts into this show? Even Maggie.

He refused to turn his back on her. He'd be the better person.

Not terribly difficult when she wasn't quite the person he'd thought she was.

He'd thought he loved her.

And that kiss . . .

An older gentleman in a suit entered, a member of the hotel's staff. "Ah, you're still here, Mr. Duke."

"Just leaving." Prescott straightened up. "Thank you for everything. It was wonderful. Please make sure it's all on my bill."

"Actually, you have a telephone call. The gentleman has called several times this evening. I've told him you were hosting a party, but he's insistent."

Prescott glanced at his watch. Who would call at nine o'clock?

He followed the gentleman to the lobby, entered the phone booth, and picked up the receiver. "Prescott Duke."

"What do you think you're doing?"

Prescott's eyebrows sprang high. "Melvin?" He'd never heard that tone from his agent.

"You pitched to Ruben? After I told you to let it go?" A jab of a punch to Prescott's ear.

He sank back against the wall of the booth. Mel thought Prescott had gone behind his back. "I didn't mean—"

"Come on, Press. It was handwritten. I saw two misspellings on the first page—and I'm not that good a speller. How could you show that to him?"

Maggie had typed it, cleaned up his spelling. "That wasn't what I—"

"You made me look ridiculous." A cross punch to Prescott's heart. "My actors begging for work? Pitching half-baked scripts to producers?"

Combination punches pummeled his gut. Half-baked? Was that what Val had said?

Melvin cussed. "It takes time to build credibility in this town. Producers know when I come to them with talent, it's good. The right man for the right part. The right script for the right studio. Then . . . Press, what got into you?"

The story. The story got into him. A low groan flowed from his battered gut.

A sigh from Melvin. "It's all right. I smoothed things over with Val. Told him you were going through a rough patch, but you'd get through. He'd only read a few pages anyway, so no harm done."

Prescott rubbed at the pain in his stomach. If his script had been any good, Val would have read more than a few pages.

"Listen, Press. I know all about rough patches. But you've got to take my advice. You always have—I've always liked that about you."

"I'm sorry."

"All forgiven. Now, first thing in the new year, come to the office. We'll talk, find some hobbies for you. Birdwatching, stamp collecting, something. We'll figure it out."

The pain drained away, leaving nothing but nothingness.

TEN

On the tenth day of Christmas my true love sent to me . . .
ten lords a-leaping.

FRIDAY, DECEMBER 10, 1943

The women's dressing room crackled with happy tension as the ladies applied stage makeup, zipped red velvet dresses, and buckled ankle straps of high-heeled tap shoes.

Maggie's breath skittered all over, and she glanced at her image in a lightbulb-ringed mirror. Even a new red suit, rouge, and powder couldn't conceal her pale cheeks and red nose after a tear-soaked night.

Vi hugged Maggie's shoulders, and her green eyes sparkled. "Don't worry. The show will be swell."

Those eyes would sparkle even more when she saw her Frank.

All night long, Maggie had wrestled with her plan. But it was a good plan, she knew it. Soon Prescott would see.

If he even came.

Maggie forced a big smile. "All right, ladies. Twenty minutes until showtime. Head to the wings as soon as possible. I'll check on the men."

If Prescott didn't come, what would she do? How could she cover his many roles?

She knocked on the door of the men's dressing room. "Good evening, gentlemen. Is everyone here?"

"We'd better be," Albert called out.

"Great. Time to take your places."

The door opened, and the men filed out in matching white shirts, black trousers, and green velvet jerkins. They looked fabulous.

Even Prescott, who came out last. He paused beside her, in profile, his face impassive. "You thought I wouldn't come."

Maggie kept her tone as calm as his. "It occurred to me."

"The show must go on." His gaze slid to her, lukewarm, and he strode away.

Maggie clutched at her belly. She could have handled hot anger or cold rejection. But lukewarm? As if she wasn't worthy of regard. As if she'd disappointed him.

For two months, he'd been more than the star of her show. He'd been her partner, as they fed off each other's ideas. He'd been her friend, as they encouraged each other. And for a few short minutes, they'd been in love, kissing with abandon.

Now he'd withdrawn his encouragement, his support, and his love. Because of his worries, his fixation on what might go wrong. She was better off without him.

So why did she feel as if she'd been sawn in two?

Prescott was right about one thing though. The show must go on.

Maggie drew herself tall and went to the prompt desk in the

wings to stage left. There lay her script for the entire show, filled with notations on blocking and cues.

Tonight, with her role as director finished, she'd serve as stage manager, while Ria managed stage right.

Beyond the heaviness of the curtain, the band played Christmas music and conversation hummed. Out there, in the boxes along the theater's circular walls, sat those admirals and civic leaders. Mr. Anderson planned to sit center front with the USO leaders.

And with Grandpa.

Maggie's face crumpled. At least Grandpa loved her.

Bright lights reduced the audience to black silhouettes. Yet each man in the theater was far more than a silhouette, and Prescott wouldn't abandon them.

"Good evening, San Diego," he said with a grin. "My name is Prescott Duke, a name you may remember from film, a voice you may remember from film. But the face? Ah, I'm afraid I was burned in a bus accident on the way to Army training camp. I guess I should have joined the Navy."

Nervous laughter rose from the blackened rows.

Prescott raised one arm. "USO-Camp Shows is proud to present 'The Twelve Days and Twelfth Night of Christmas.' We hope to bring you a little music, a few laughs, and even a bit of culture if it doesn't kill you."

More laughter, more relaxed.

"So here we are, about to spend the holidays in sunny San Diego."

Now laughter poured like the rain that had fallen all day.

"Sandy beaches instead of sleigh rides. Palm trees instead of pine. Green instead of white. What would our partridge in a pear tree sing if she were assigned to the United States Navy's Repair Base, San Diego? May I introduce our lovely partridge, Miss Violet Lane?" And he sang, "'On the first day of Christmas my true love sent to me a partridge in a pear tree.'"

He made a sweeping gesture to stage right as he backed off to stage left.

The band played the introduction to "White Christmas," and Vi came onstage, trailing her hand around the trunk of the fake pear tree. After a swing lowered from the "branch" at the top of the stage, Vi took her perch, and she swung and sang in her melodious soprano.

All night, Prescott had debated with himself. He'd wanted to warn Vi before the show, let her know Frank was alive, prepare her so she could rejoice at Frank's arrival.

But what if the shock undid her? What if she was in no shape to go onstage?

The show could be ruined. That wouldn't be fair to the cast, the audience, or even to Maggie. Even though she was making a mistake, she didn't deserve to lose her job over it. And Mr. Curtis certainly didn't deserve to lose his home and dog.

Maggie stood in the prompt corner as the cast lined up in the wings for "Winter Wonderland." She met his gaze, her face puckered, and she glanced away.

An ache grew in his chest.

Sometime before dawn, he'd decided not to tell Vi. He'd chosen not to reveal the truth for fear of harming the show. He'd chosen one potential harm over another. Was he any better than Maggie?

What if she'd considered the same factors? Last night he hadn't delved much before she'd run off. Had he leapt to conclusions about her placing entertainment above people? For the past two months, compassion had shone at the core of her character. Had he been hasty in judging her?

Vi finished her solo and flitted off like a bird. Applause erupted, pierced by whistles. Her star quality had shone, and Prescott went to center stage. "Isn't she wonderful? Miss Violet Lane."

When the applause faded, Prescott sang, "'On the second day of Christmas my true love sent to me two turtle doves.'"

He ambled backward to his mark for the song. "You know what they say about turtle doves—they're together for life. All around me this Christmas, I see couples in love, enjoying San Diego's winter wonderland of sunshine and seashore. But will I ever find my own turtle dove?" He heard the pang in his own voice. No acting required.

The band launched into "Winter Wonderland." Greta and Freddie strutted out stage left, Nan and Ferdy stage right, their feet tapping to the rhythm as they danced. Both couples paused on their marks, performed their little solos, and pranced offstage.

Flirty, perky, energetic, and Prescott's smile rose as he sang. No acting required.

How he'd enjoyed the past two months, working and laughing with these men and women. He refused to let last night's devastation knock him out for the count. He'd learned too much.

He'd lost Maggie and soon he'd lose contact with this cast, but he would make new friendships. He'd lost his purpose of writing, but he'd find a new aim or create one.

No matter what, he would use his hurt to help people.

Never had the cast performed so well, and a tiny laugh bubbled through the persistent damp grief in Maggie's chest.

"'Ten lords a-leaping,'" Prescott sang, and the men played leapfrog onto the stage as the drums pounded and the audience laughed.

Something had changed in Prescott during "Winter Wonderland," brightening his voice and enlivening his demeanor, and his brightness and liveliness had flowed out to the cast.

What was that something? It had arisen without any encouragement from her. In the middle of the aching realization that he didn't want or need her glowed an ember of contentment. He would be fine without her, and she did want the best for him.

"'Nine ladies dancing,'" and the women pirouetted onstage for their bows.

Sure, there had been some glitches in the show. Carol forgot a few lines, but only a Shakespeare expert would have missed them. Some dance steps were botched. Two missed cues, easily smoothed over.

"'Eight maids a-milking.'" Barbara and Nan reprised their comedy duo as a milkmaid chasing a cow who didn't want to be milked and only wanted to "jingle her bells."

The audience cheered for the women. They'd applauded the songs, whistled at the dances, and even laughed at Shakespeare's wit.

This was what she'd dreamed of—to bring smiles to men who might be lonely, broken, or afraid. To show them what their service meant to the American people.

From the prompt desk, Maggie resisted the temptation to peek out to the audience.

How proud Grandpa would be. And Mr. Anderson. The USO would see that single women could be entrusted with responsibility. Her job was secure. Papa would relent and not sell Grandpa's house. All would be well.

"'Five gold rings.'" Greta performed an acrobatic backbend through her big rings.

If all was well, why did Maggie have a hopping sensation in her belly?

Prescott. He stood center stage, his smile crinkling his face as he sang.

Losing him hurt. But disappointing him hurt possibly even more.

What if he was right?

From the beginning, she'd had second thoughts about Frank and Vi's reunion, but only about delaying until opening night. Not once had she imagined Frank and Vi doing anything but falling tearfully into each other's arms.

What if they . . . didn't? What if it were all doom and gloom as Prescott imagined?

Would a private reunion have been better?

"Happy Holiday" resounded from the stage, and Maggie blinked at the sight of the cast holding hands in alternating red and green costumes. Where had the rest of the curtain call gone?

That meant Frank was already in the lobby with Ria standing at the lobby door.

It was too late to change plans now, and Maggie huffed away her misgivings.

The applause died down, and Vi introduced Maggie so she could dismiss the sailors to their buses. "Now a word from our director, Miss Margaret Oliver."

The cast cheered for her.

Maggie's eyes filled. She gave herself a little shake, and she came onstage applauding her cast, avoiding Prescott's gaze.

She stopped center stage. "May I have the house lights, please?"

Not in the show plan, but soon the house lights came on and the stage lights dimmed.

In the front row, Grandpa beamed at her, as did Mr. Anderson.

Maggie smiled at the sea of blue uniforms. "On behalf of the USO, I want to thank our cast, the city of San Diego, and the United States Navy."

More applause, and Maggie drew a deep breath. "Now I have a Christmas surprise. In *Twelfth Night*, Viola was separated from her brother Sebastian, lost at sea and presumed dead. I'm sad to say our own Violet Lane lost her beloved fiancé at sea."

Sad murmurs from the audience, and a pained gasp from Vi.

Maggie gave her an apologetic look and turned back to the audience. "I'm pleased to present Miss Lane's very own Sebastian—Petty Officer Frank Sebastian. Mrs. Fernandez?" She nodded to Ria.

At the back door, Ria gaped at her.

"Frank?" Vi murmured behind her. "No, he—he's . . ."

Carol flew to Vi's side and wrapped an arm around her waist.

A comforting smile for Vi, and Maggie repeated her request. "Mrs. Fernandez?"

Still gaping, Ria opened the door.

Wearing his dress blues, Frank entered the theater with a questioning look for Ria.

"Petty Officer Sebastian, I have a joyous Christmas surprise for you." Maggie gestured to Vi, slumped at Carol's side.

Frank's mouth fell open. "Vernice?"

"No." Vi shook her head over and over. "No, he—he's dead."

Two lurching steps down the aisle. "Vernice?"

"Frank? You—you're alive?"

Maggie stepped aside, her heart full. Now they'd run to each other.

"You're alive?" Vi clutched Carol's arm, and a strange note elevated her voice. Anger? "You mean to tell me you've been alive all this time?"

"I—I've been looking." Frank's arms rose, open, reaching. "I didn't know where—"

"I thought you were dead." Vi's voice climbed, quaked. "Almost two years. I've been grieving all this time, and you—I thought you loved me."

"Oh no," Maggie whispered. This wasn't supposed to happen.

"All this time." Vi's gaze swung to Maggie, her nostrils flared, and she shoved away from Carol and staggered backstage.

Gasps and murmurs filled the circular theater.

Maggie's feet glued to the floorboards, her jaw drooped, her lungs failed to breathe, her heart—was it even beating?

"Vernice!" Frank darted down the aisle, then slammed to a stop. He glanced around the theater, where five hundred pairs of eyes pinned on him. His face stretched long, and he clapped one hand to his belly. Clapped one hand over his mouth.

Turned and sprinted to the lobby.

Breath seared its way into Maggie's lungs. Was he going to be sick?

An appalled hush sucked the air from the theater.

Maggie couldn't move. Couldn't speak. What had she done?

Now those five hundred pairs of eyes turned on her. Grandpa stared at her, aghast. So did Mr. Anderson.

What on earth had she done?

Prescott had wanted Maggie to realize she was wrong—but not like this. Never like this.

Maggie stumbled backward, bumped into his chest.

His hands rose to brace her—but stopped.

She spun to him. Her face . . . dissolved. She brushed past him and ran backstage.

The mumbles in the audience turned to rumbles.

"Press." Albert tugged Prescott's sleeve. "You've got to do something."

What could he do? All he knew was he couldn't leave the audience with a foul taste in their mouths, couldn't let the cast's hard work fall to pieces.

Praying for the right words, Prescott raised one hand to quiet the audience. "Gentlemen, I'm afraid that when show people are in the room, you have to expect the dramatic."

A great quieting and relaxing settled in.

"That isn't how we want to close this evening," he said. "We came together tonight to bring you Christmas cheer. For those of you who celebrate Christmas, this is a season to rejoice over the birth of our Lord and the wonders of his love. For those who don't celebrate, it's still a season of joy and wonder and love. Would you please join me in singing 'Joy to the World'? A cappella," he told the startled band director.

Prescott waved his hand like a choir director and launched into the carol. Deep, rough voices of men billowed through the theater.

Ria strode down the aisle, waving at him.

"Albert, can you lead?" Prescott whispered to him, and Albert nodded and took over.

Prescott met Ria at the corner of the stage.

With her dark eyes piercing, she stuck a piece of paper in his hand. "Frank and Maggie were supposed to dismiss the men to the buses."

They were both gone.

"Read that from the stage." Ria pointed to the paper. "One bus at a time. I'll direct them out from the lobby."

"I can do that. Thanks, Ria."

Prescott returned to finish the third verse, then he stepped to the edge of the stage. "Thank you, everyone. Good night and Merry Christmas."

The cast bowed, and the curtain lowered behind him.

"Please listen for your bus to be dismissed. If you arrived on bus one, please head to the lobby. Follow Mrs. Fernandez." He gestured to Ria, who waved from the back door. "Everyone else, please remain seated."

In the front row, Mr. Curtis pushed himself to standing and hobbled to the stage. "Prescott!"

"Yes?" He squatted down.

The older man's brown eyes pierced even more than Ria's. "Go after Maggie."

Prescott suppressed a grimace.

"She'll need to talk to someone."

Not him. Prescott raised one hand to tell Mr. Curtis to wait.

He rose, dismissed bus two, and squatted again. "She won't want to talk to me."

White eyebrows lowered. "I heard her crying last night."

Prescott's grimace broke through. "We argued."

"Regardless, she needs to talk, and you're the best one."

"I can't go into the women's dressing room, and the ladies will do a much better job of listening to her."

"Not the dressing room. The Lily Pond."

"The Lily Pond?"

"She always said it'd be a dramatic place for a good cry."

Prescott had heard her say that very thing. He stood and called for bus three.

"If you won't go," Mr. Curtis said, "I will."

In the pouring rain in the blacked-out night? "No, you can't go."

"Then you will? Thank you. That's my bus." Mr. Curtis took Mr. Anderson's arm and made his way down the aisle.

Prescott's jaw fell open. He couldn't go to Maggie. Why should he? Let her cry alone. She'd rejected his advice and hurt two friends. Why should he help her?

"Bus four." A niggling sensation clawed in his gut. What was it he'd said to himself last night? About refusing to turn his back on her?

He hadn't done so. He'd come to the show and performed his best.

Was Mr. Curtis's request any different? Asking Prescott to lay aside his pain and help someone?

But Maggie had hurt a lot of people.

"Bus five." The lines of "Joy to the World" repeated in his head. The world had received its King—and crucified him. Yet Jesus showed mercy.

So should Prescott. He groaned and kept dismissing the sailors.

Two trucks would arrive at ten thirty to take the cast to the streetcar terminal. If nothing else, Maggie needed to be on that truck, or the USO would be in trouble with the Navy.

After the last sailor left the theater, Prescott shoved through the curtain and went to the men's dressing room. He ignored the chatter, removed his jerkin so the velvet wouldn't be ruined in the rain, changed into street shoes, and put on his coat and hat.

Outside, he charged forward, his head low, his hat a shield against the rain. Through the overcast, an almost-full moon barely illuminated the path through the arcade in front of a Spanish Colonial building and across a plaza with raindrops plinking on the pavement.

At the end of another arcade, he reached the Lily Pond. Maybe Maggie wouldn't be there. Then he could say he'd done his best and leave.

Close to the Botanical Building, a walkway divided the upper and lower ponds. A hunched figure sat on the railing.

Prescott grumbled. "All right, Lord. Since this is your idea, let me know what to say."

As he came closer, the Botanical Building emerged from the mist of rain, long and domed like a railroad station. The rain would be pelting through the thin redwood laths forming the roof.

As he reached the walkway, the sound of weeping beat out the sound of raindrops pummeling his hat.

Prescott leaned back against the broad railing, several feet from Maggie.

Her head jerked up. "Oh no. Why'd you come? To lord it over me?" Only distress distorted her voice, not anger.

Prescott didn't intend to talk much. Mr. Curtis had instructed him to listen. "Your grandpa told me to come. Besides, you have only forty-five minutes to catch your ride home."

"I'll walk home." Her voice wavered. "I deserve it."

Sighing, Prescott crossed his arms and tucked his hands under his armpits to keep a little dry. He was in no mood for more theatrics.

"Go ahead," she cried. "Say, 'I told you so.'"

He shook his head. He didn't need to say it.

Her back and shoulders curved low. "You should say it. You were right, and I was wrong. Horribly wrong. I wanted a spectacle, and oh, I got one. A spectacular fiasco."

Raindrops created little spouts as they hit the pond. He didn't want to look at Maggie. Certainly didn't want to feel sorry for her.

"Poor Vi," she said with a sob. "Poor Frank."

At least she hadn't said, "Poor me."

"I wanted them to have a happy ending." She covered her eyes with her hands. "Now they'll never speak to each other again. And I embarrassed them—publicly. It was nothing—nothing like I imagined, and it was even worse than you imagined."

Prescott released another sigh. She was right about that.

"I'm sorry, Press. You warned me, and I didn't listen. Why didn't I listen? Grandpa told me not to meddle, told me if I'm keeping secrets, I'm meddling. But no, I told myself it was no different than a surprise party or a Christmas gift. But it was meddling. And I ruined their lives." True remorse quivered in her voice, and she chewed on a thumbnail.

Why would Prescott need to speak when she was telling herself everything he might have said—and more?

"I was trying to listen to God." Limp dark strands covered her cheeks. "I was. I was praying about this. I really was, Press."

That niggling again, and words built in his head and flowed over his tongue. "Were you praying that your plan would work? Or were you asking God whether your plan was wise?"

Maggie lifted her head and shoved aside tendrils of hair. In the darkness, her eyes and mouth formed large dark circles. Then she sobbed and hunched over her knees again.

"Come on," Prescott said. "Let's get you out of the rain."

"No. I chose entertainment over people, just as you said. Same as I always do. I'm the one who got Rose sick. My little sister got meningitis because I ignored my mother and played with her when I was sick."

Prescott arched one eyebrow. He hadn't heard this part of the story.

Her teeth clicked on her thumbnail. "My parents never blamed me, said I was only six years old. But I was old enough to listen, old enough to know I'd ruined my sister's life."

A twisting in Prescott's gut. What a heavy load to carry. "You were little. How were you to know?"

She waved him off. "And now—why didn't I listen to Grandpa? To you? I'll lose my job and rightly so."

Prescott groaned. "It may not be as bad as all that. If you apologize—"

"No, no." She clapped her hands on her knees and sat up straight. "I won't make them fire me. I'll resign."

"Don't be hasty."

"It's the right thing to do. The USO trusted me, and I abused their trust. Besides, if I resign, maybe Vi will agree to perform.

You and Ria—you can manage the show. Everything ran smoothly tonight. You don't need me."

Not true, but she had a point about Vi, and he grimaced.

"Oh, Grandpa." She sagged back down over her knees. "What am I going to do?"

"Get a job."

She glanced up. "Pardon?"

"The aircraft factories in San Diego are hiring. If you can't get a job as a secretary, there are training classes at the vocational school right here in Balboa Park."

"The Ford Building . . ." One of the few not occupied by the Navy.

Prescott planned to apply first thing in January. Maybe a factory could figure out what to do with strong arms and disfigured-but-willing hands. "Pays better than the USO, I'm sure. It may not be your dream job, but—"

"But it'll keep Grandpa in his home with Tobias. And that is my true dream."

Her heart really was in the right place, and Prescott fought against the softening inside. "Come on. You need to catch your ride." He pushed away from the railing but didn't offer a helping hand.

Maggie awkwardly swung her legs over the railing and hopped down to the walkway. "I need to find Vi. She deserves an apology."

Prescott led the way, staying a good four feet away from Maggie, and they entered the shelter of an arcade.

"Oh, Vi. Oh, Frank." Maggie clapped her hands to her cheeks. "I know they still love each other. Vi—she was so angry with him. But how could Frank have found her? She changed her name."

Prescott dug his hands into his coat pockets. "Vi is a reasonable woman. She's upset now, but—"

"What should I do, Press?" Her eyes looked wild in the dim light. "I'll listen to you this time, I promise. Or should I keep my nose out of it?"

Tempting to accept the last suggestion, but he shook his head. "Talk to Vi. She may not be ready to listen, but if she truly loves Frank—"

"She does. I know she does."

"How about I talk to Frank tomorrow? Ria can help me find him."

"Yes, man to man. That's good. Please apologize to him for me. He looked sick to his stomach. The poor man."

Indeed. A man's pride didn't bear humiliation like that well. They crossed the plaza, and Prescott tipped the brim of his hat low. "If they both want to see each other, we'll set something up. Quiet. Private."

"All right. That sounds wise."

Prescott sloshed through a puddle. Thank goodness he had spare shoes in the hotel.

"Press?" she said. Soft. Tremulous. "You said 'we.' We'll set it up."

Prescott stopped in his tracks and fixed a strong gaze on her. "Not like that."

"Oh my goodness." Both hands flew to her mouth. "I'm sorry. I didn't mean—I know—I'll stop talking now."

He plodded forward. Eventually he would forgive her. She was truly remorseful and wanted to make amends, and he admired that.

But romance would be asking too much.

ELEVEN

On the eleventh day of Christmas my true love sent to me . . . eleven pipers piping.

Backstage, Maggie's shoes made wet, squishing sounds, and she suppressed a shudder.

At the door to the women's dressing room, Prescott stopped without facing her. "Can you have Ria call my hotel tomorrow morning so she can help me meet with Frank?"

"Yes." Maggie's voice shook with cold despite her efforts. "I'm meeting with her and Mr. Anderson in the morning to discuss the show." That was when she'd resign.

Rain had darkened Prescott's khaki raincoat to the color of mud. "After I talk to Frank, I'll have Ria call your house with the plan. Since you won't be here tomorrow."

No, she wouldn't. "Thank you."

A brisk nod, and Prescott strode toward the men's dressing room. Not hot or cold or even lukewarm—just *there*. Present.

Why had he been so kind after she'd treated him and Frank and Vi so horribly? Not only had he performed in the show—and well—but he'd searched for her at the Lily Pond. He'd listened to her and helped her find solutions—solutions to problems she had created.

His kindness only intensified the ache of losing him, only made her love him more.

Behind the door, women's voices mumbled.

Now Maggie had to face Vi—face all of them.

Droplets from her hair dribbled down her neck and joined the sodden mess of blouse and suit clammy against her skin.

"Lord, help me know what to say," she whispered. "For Vi's sake."

She opened the door, and nine women stared at her.

Half a dozen sprang to the door. "You have some nerve."

"How dare you show your face?"

"Just go away."

"I want to apologize to Vi." Maggie's voice was swept away in the flood of accusations. Rightful accusations.

"Pipe down!" Greta's voice climbed over the din.

The ladies spun to face her.

"Pipe down." Greta stood with hands on hips. "Maggie's trying to apologize. Don't you think Vi deserves an apology?"

Nan flung a hand in Maggie's direction. "Yeah, but Maggie doesn't deserve Vi's forgiveness."

"Certainly not." Carol glared at Maggie. "Just leave, would you?"

Maggie winced and folded shivering arms over her drenched midriff.

"Let her speak," Greta said. "Carol, wasn't Maggie patient when you didn't learn your lines? And Nan, didn't she help when you were hysterical about your costume?"

Reluctant grumbles.

"I'm not here for forgiveness." Maggie paused while her teeth chattered. "I was wrong, and I have no excuse. I just want to tell Vi how terribly sorry I am."

"Let her." Vi's voice rose from behind the protective wall of women.

Still glowering at Maggie, the ladies parted.

Vi sat in a chair in her street clothes, hugging herself, her eyes a very un-festive mix of red and green. Her mouth puckered. "What were you thinking?"

Maggie sank into a chair beside Vi. She didn't want to excuse her inexcusable behavior. "I'm so sorry. I—I wanted to give you and Frank a happy reunion. It never occurred to me—"

"You knew Frank was alive?" With her stage makeup scrubbed off, Vi's lovely face was marred by red splotches and tear tracks. "Why didn't you tell me?"

Gritting her teeth, Maggie tried to dry her hands on her sodden skirt. "I was wrong to keep it from you, wrong to make a public spectacle, and wrong—so very wrong—to hurt two friends."

A scoffing sound from Carol. "I'll say."

Maggie sucked in a breath to stem her tears. "I see now what a horrible shock it was for you. And—and I embarrassed Frank."

Vi's mottled cheeks agitated. "He hates to be in the limelight. Oh, Frank. Oh no."

"He still loves you," Maggie said in a soft voice. "He did look for you, but—"

"But I changed my name." Vi pressed her hands over her eyes, and her Southern accent emerged. "He was looking for Vernice Lingenfelter, not Violet Lane. Oh, Frank."

"Don't make excuses for him," Nan said. "He could have asked your family."

"I don't have family." A muffled wail rose. "I never told anyone back home where I went. Just up and ran to Hollywood, changed my name. Poor Frank. He was searching for me? What have I done? He'll never want to see me again."

Maggie leaned closer. "Prescott will talk to him tomorrow. If Frank agrees, would you like to meet with him? Someplace quiet and private."

Vi bobbled a nod. "I can't believe he's alive. All this time . . . oh, Frank."

One more issue needed to be addressed, and Maggie drew a breath into her shuddering chest. "I'll understand if you can't perform in the show tomorrow—or ever."

"I'm dropping out of the show too." Carol crossed her arms.

That was worse than Maggie imagined—again—and her breath hopped around.

"Don't be silly, Carol." Greta rolled her eyes. "You have a contract."

"I don't care. I can't bear to look at her." Yet Carol did look at her—with contempt.

"You won't have to look at me. I won't be here for the rest of the run." Mentioning her resignation might look like a ploy for sympathy, and she refused. "Prescott and Ria will manage the show. Greta, could you help stage left?"

"You didn't hear me." Carol's eyes formed icicle daggers. "I'm dropping out, and the rest of you should too."

"No, Carol." Vi lowered her hands. "This isn't about Maggie. We aren't doing this show for her. We never were. We're doing it for those sailors and soldiers and Marines. I'll be here tomorrow, and you'd better be here too. All of you."

Carol lowered her chin and mumbled her agreement.

Tomorrow they'd come, and the show would go on.

Without Maggie.

SATURDAY, DECEMBER 11, 1943

Soft rain, a chilled breeze, and an opportunity recklessly thrown away. With an umbrella overhead and an empty suitcase in hand, Maggie paused outside the USO-Army-Navy YMCA building. Then she trudged up granite steps.

Time to pay the piper.

After she checked in her raincoat and umbrella, she crossed the tiled lobby, passing Mrs. Laverne at the front desk with a civil exchange of "good morning." Mrs. Laverne must not have heard about last night's disaster, or she'd be gloating.

The morning meeting had been scheduled to discuss opening night and any changes needed for the upcoming performances. Never once had Maggie imagined she'd resign at the meeting.

Maggie made her way down the hallway. Apparently her imagination had serious limitations.

If only she'd listened to Prescott's concerns about the reunion and to Grandpa's warnings about keeping secrets. If only she'd asked God for wisdom rather than success. She might have avoided heartbreak for Frank and Vi. For Prescott. For Grandpa.

A wave of dizziness, and Maggie braced herself against the wall and caught her breath. "'O time, thou must untangle this, not I; It is too hard a knot for me t' untie!'"

Yet she was the one who'd tied a knot of Shakespearean proportions, and she was the one who had to pick at that knot.

Poor Grandpa. He'd turned ashen when she'd told him she

planned to resign. Later today, she would apply for work at Consolidated Aircraft. If she couldn't find a high-paying job before Papa arrived from Iowa, Grandpa would lose his house.

Grandpa had said he'd make do. But he'd held Tobias even tighter as he'd said it.

Maggie squared her shoulders and forged upstairs and into her office. She set her suitcase on a chair and opened it to fill with her belongings.

Cheerful voices in the hallway, and Mr. Anderson entered the office with Ria.

Before her courage ran out, Maggie straightened her blue suit jacket, the one Grandpa said made her eyes look as blue as Grandma's. "Mr. Anderson, I apologize for last night."

"Last night?" His frown tugged down the corners of his mustache.

"I let down your confidence in me, let down the USO. And Ria, I let you down too. I let down the whole cast, the Navy, and most of all, I let down two friends. I created a fiasco because I prized spectacle over people. I am resigning from my position immediately."

"A fiasco?" He glanced at Ria. "That hiccup at the end?"

"More than a hiccup." A growl entered Ria's voice.

"It was entirely my fault, Mr. Anderson." Maggie firmed her jaw. "Mrs. Fernandez knew nothing about my plan, and I take full responsibility."

Ria's mouth shifted to one side. "Frank is pretty upset."

"Vi is too, but she realizes Frank could never have found her after she changed her name. She wants to meet with Frank." Maggie took one step toward her assistant. "Could you call Prescott? Could you help him meet with Frank? Tell Prescott that Vi has agreed to see Frank. That might help when Prescott talks to him."

Ria's mouth softened. "I'd be glad to. Those young people deserve another chance."

"They do. Thank you." Maggie picked up a framed photograph of Grandpa and Grandma from her desk and tucked it into her suitcase. "I'll be out of the office in a few minutes."

"I don't see why," Mr. Anderson said. "Mr. Duke smoothed things over, and everyone loved the show."

Maggie straightened up and set one hand on the desk for balance. "Mr. Duke did what?"

Ria shrugged. "He joked about how dramatic show people are, made a nice little speech, and led everyone in singing 'Joy to the World.'"

He'd done that? The ache of losing him dug even deeper into her chest, as if anything remained in her chest at all.

"As I said, all smoothed over." Mr. Anderson took a seat and tugged down his suit jacket. "Everyone raved about the show, from the admirals to the enlisted seamen. Outstanding. Best show they've ever seen. Best I've ever seen. They'll be talking about it for months."

"I'm glad." Moisture blurred Maggie's vision. "It'll continue without me."

"Without you?" Ria's black eyebrows jammed together. "We can't do it without you."

"Yes, you can. As emcee, Prescott keeps the show running. You can manage stage right, and Greta can help stage left."

"That won't work." Ria shot a glance at Mr. Anderson. "Who will manage when Greta's onstage? We need Miss Oliver."

"I agree," Mr. Anderson said.

"No, no." Maggie's hand fluttered to her belly. "You don't understand. The ladies are furious with me. I promised them I wouldn't be there. They might not perform if I'm there."

A grumble from Ria, and she rolled her eyes. "I'll talk to them."

"But they—"

"They'll listen to me." Ria swung a searing glance from Maggie to Mr. Anderson. "Miss Oliver is the reason the show is so good. You'd better not accept her resignation."

Mr. Anderson adjusted his glasses. "I had no intention of doing so."

Maggie's head shook back and forth. "But I don't—"

"Nonsense," Mr. Anderson said. "No harm was done to the reputation of the USO. As for your little lapse in judgment—"

"It wasn't a little lapse, sir. It was a great big gaping hole."

Mr. Anderson clasped his hands over his knees and studied her with his head tipped to one side. "Will you do it again?"

"Never, sir. But—"

"But you took responsibility and you're trying to make things better." He patted his knees. "Now, shall we start this meeting? You both need to get to the theater by eleven, right?"

"Right." Ria gave Maggie a challenging look and plopped into her usual chair.

Maggie's chair was occupied by her open suitcase, and she stared down at Grandpa and Grandma's smiling faces.

She didn't deserve this job. But Grandpa deserved to stay in his home.

It was all she'd wanted for Christmas.

A gift of mercy, and she accepted it.

BEVERLY HILLS
WEDNESDAY, DECEMBER 15, 1943

Prescott's footsteps reverberated in the palatial parlor.

On his day off from performing, he'd gone home to Beverly Hills.

No, not home. A house. Pristine Streamline Moderne. Immaculate white and chrome. Every piece of furniture and art chosen by the designer hired by the studio to create a habitation for their image of Prescott Duke.

He'd felt far more at home on the old sofa in Bill Curtis's home with a scruffy dog at his feet and Maggie puttering in the kitchen.

A vise clamped his heart, and he sank to the piano bench as Charles Anthony had done on his darkest day.

Prescott held his six remaining digits over the keyboard and plunked out fragments of a tune. Before his accident, he'd been taking piano lessons and enjoying them.

Unlike Charles, Prescott could no longer play. But also unlike Charles, he hadn't lost everything.

The USO shows had continued over the past four days. The performances felt more subdued, but few would notice.

Each day, Maggie slipped into the theater and did her job in an unobtrusive way. Prescott had never seen anyone more humbled, more contrite, more chastened. He loved her more than ever. But he didn't trust her with his heart.

An off-key chord assaulted his ears. He grabbed his attaché case and went to the garage, where he started his car.

He drove past more palatial homes, each isolated behind gates from the neighbors, then down Sunset Boulevard.

Tonight would be difficult.

On Saturday morning, Ria had taken him to Balboa Park to meet with Frank Sebastian, who very much wanted to see Vi again.

Maggie had proposed a quiet home-cooked dinner for the couple. Since Ria's house overflowed with family, only Maggie's house was available. Maggie planned to cook dinner then retreat out of sight while someone else served.

Mr. Curtis had plans for the evening. So did Ria. That left Prescott.

He didn't mind serving. He did mind seeing Maggie at a place where they'd shared many pleasant hours.

Before long, Prescott arrived at Melvin's office on Wilshire Boulevard, and Edna ushered him in even though he didn't have an appointment.

Melvin rose from his desk with his eyebrows arched high. "Press?"

"I wanted you to see that I'm fine." He offered a smile and a handshake.

Melvin's chair creaked as he returned to sitting. "Listen, I'm sorry for how this all shook out. I could have handled it better."

Prescott took his customary chair and opened his attaché case. "I could have handled it better too. I want you to know I never meant to go over your head, only to get another opinion before giving up writing. If Val had liked the script, I would have worked with you as always. Now, I don't know legal jargon, but I believe my contract with you is only as a performer." He handed Melvin the document.

Melvin's lips went tight. "Correct."

"I would have needed a new contract—or an addendum—for you to represent me as a writer. Which is what I would have wanted. However, when I spoke to Val as a writer, I didn't violate the letter or the heart of our contract."

Something shifted in Melvin's dark eyes—from his usual fatherly benevolence to the respectful way he looked at directors and producers. He cleared his throat. "That's correct."

"I know you're concerned about my image, your image, and the studio's ability to sell film rights. That's why I would have used a pen name—Joseph P. Duke."

Melvin murmured his approval.

Prescott opened his hand for his contract and tucked the document into his attaché case. "That's the name I'll use in my new life."

"Your new life?"

"I refuse to be a hermit. I need to work. I'll apply for factory jobs here in LA." San Diego carried too many memories. "I'll go back to being Joe. Not Joe Prescott—I'm not that man anymore. But I'm not really Prescott Duke anymore either."

"You'll always be—"

"Prescott Duke has a big fancy house in Beverly Hills. I plan to sell some of the art, rent out the house, and buy something smaller near my new job. Nothing fancy, but it'll be mine."

Melvin leaned back in his chair, tapped his fingers on his armrests, and scrutinized Prescott. "This is a new side of you."

"A bright side?" A wry chuckle broke out at the memory of Maggie posing onstage, showing Prescott a new path. "Recently someone told me if you can't find a bright side, make one. That's what I'm doing."

With a grunt, Melvin pushed his large frame out of his chair. "I believe you'll do just that. I wish you the best."

"Thank you." He shook his agent's hand and said goodbye to Edna.

Outside on Wilshire Boulevard in cool sunshine, he walked a few blocks to Valentine Ruben's office.

When the secretary admitted Prescott, Val pumped his hand. "Good to see you. I was surprised to see you'd made an appointment."

"I wanted to see you for two reasons." Prescott took the offered chair across from Val's carved mahogany desk. "First, I'd like to pick up my script if you haven't thrown it away."

Val frowned and sat in a chair that dwarfed him. "I still have it."

"Good." Although Maggie had created a carbon copy, Prescott wanted the original for a souvenir. "I also came to apologize. I ignored Melvin's advice to give up writing, and I did what I thought best. I also took advantage of our friendship. I'm sorry, Val."

"Not at all. I just wish you'd reconsider."

"Reconsider what?"

"Giving up this project. Melvin was in a state, and I never got a chance to tell him how much I like your script."

Prescott's vision swam, and he blinked a few times. "Pardon?"

"I'd only read the first scene when I called him. But afterward, I kept reading. Couldn't stop. It's the best I've read in years. Any chance you'd reconsider?"

Thoughts circled Prescott's brain, colliding with each other. Nothing made sense. "You—you liked it?"

Val shrugged narrow shoulders. "It's got rough spots, needs work. I'd hook you up with a writer."

Standard practice in Hollywood. "You're serious?"

Val inclined his head, and his dark eyes narrowed. "Are you? Are you serious about writing?"

"I—I was. I am. Are you saying you want to pursue this project?"

A chuckle, and Val leaned his elbows on his desk. "I'm saying I'd like another Oscar. You want one?"

All he could hear was Maggie's cheery voice proclaiming, "Oscars all around," and he nodded. "We need to call Melvin."

"He only read the first page, you said? Ha! I can't wait to tell the great Melvin Underwood that he was wrong." Val chuckled, picked up his phone, and dialed. "You've heard the saying 'Some are born great, some achieve greatness, and some have greatness thrust upon 'em.' Well, you're about to achieve greatness, and I've had greatness thrust upon me."

"That's Shakespeare," Prescott said. "From *Twelfth Night*."

Val stared at him and laughed. "There's more to you than meets the eye. Hey, Melvin. Val Ruben. Guess what? We need to talk."

TWELVE

On the twelfth day of Christmas my true love sent to me
. . . twelve drummers drumming.

SAN DIEGO
WEDNESDAY, DECEMBER 15, 1943

Maggie scraped mashed potatoes from the pot into a china serving bowl.

The doorbell rang.

She grimaced and slid the bowl into the oven to keep warm. That would be Prescott, right on time. If only Ria had been free tonight. Frank, Vi, and Maggie were comfortable with Ria.

Maggie was no longer comfortable with Prescott. Somehow she'd hold herself together tonight as she'd done for the past few days.

She opened the door and looked him in the eye for the first time since opening night.

His eyebrows shot high.

No wonder. He'd never seen her wearing her dowdy old dress, Grandma's ancient apron, and a kerchief about her hair—and not a speck of powder or lipstick.

She motioned him inside. "Thank you for coming."

"You're welcome." He hung his hat on the coatrack and shrugged off his coat.

Maggie strode to the dining room. "The table is set. Butter, gravy, sugar, salt and pepper, flowers in the vase. Here's a bouquet for Frank to give Vi if he didn't bring flowers himself. If he did, toss these in the kitchen."

Although her hand shook, she lit the candles. "I talked to the taxi company. Frank should arrive in ten minutes, Vi five minutes later. Here's a bell so they can ring if they need anything from you. I set up a table in Grandpa's room at the end of the hall. You can sit in there and eat your dinner. You brought a book as I asked?"

"Yes."

Maggie smoothed Grandma's embroidered Christmas tablecloth. "If you need any help, knock on my door, second on the right."

"Okay."

She edged past Prescott to the phone table in the living room. "When the evening is over, call the taxi company. Here's the number. I pray it won't be too early."

"I do too."

"Knock before you leave so I know when to clean up." In the kitchen, she tossed green beans into the pot of boiling water and set the timer. "The coffee is brewed. The roast beef and mashed potatoes are in the oven keeping warm. Here's the carving knife, plates for you and Frank and Vi. Apple pie over here, knife, plates, dessert forks. Whipped cream in the icebox." She opened the door and pointed at the bowl. "And cream for the coffee."

"Do you have any ration stamps left for December?" A teasing tone lifted his voice.

Why did that hurt even more? Recalling the easy camaraderie they'd once enjoyed. She shut the icebox. "Grandpa will. I'll get by."

"It looks very nice. You thought of everything."

A week ago, she would have agreed. "Not at all."

"Pardon?"

She picked up a dishrag and wiped a blob of mashed potato from the stovetop. "No one can think of everything, especially when people are involved."

"True," he said in a low voice.

Green beans tumbled in the roiling water. "I didn't make this new plan on my own. I asked Grandpa and Ria for advice. I prayed, and I listened. Listen, listen, listen. I've been drumming it into my head."

A murmur from Prescott.

At the sink, Maggie ran water into the potato pot and shook in soap flakes. "I always saw optimism as my strength. But at its heart—at the heart of optimism—lies a kernel of arrogance."

"Arrogance?"

Maggie pushed up her sleeves and scrubbed the pot. "It's arrogant to assume everything will turn out well just because I imagined it that way."

A creak as Prescott leaned against the open door. "You aren't alone."

"Pardon?" She started to glance his way. Stopped herself before making a huge mistake.

"Isn't pessimism similar?"

"Hardly." She dumped the soapy water into the sink and rinsed the pot.

"At the heart of pessimism lies a kernel of self-pity. Assuming everything will turn out poorly because I imagined it that way."

Maggie grabbed the dish towel and dried the pot. Her gaze turned to him, betraying her.

There was something new about him, as if he were taller, broader, wiser.

"Don't let this destroy your optimism," he said. "Only temper it."

Maggie shook her head and put the pot in the cupboard, only half dry.

"I'm serious. In your optimism, you told me to write a new script for my life. I'm glad I listened to you." No wistful longing lingered in his voice, only the peace of saying goodbye.

The timer dinged. Maggie set the colander in the sink and dumped the beans into it. "You listened." Pain seized her chest. No—she refused to cry. "If I'd listened, all of this would have been unnecessary."

The doorbell rang.

"That's Frank." Maggie slid the green beans from the colander into the vegetable bowl, untied the apron, and hung it on the hook. "I'll be in my room."

"Aren't you going to say hello?"

"I've already apologized to him through you, and I refuse to put myself in the audience tonight. As you said, Frank and Vi aren't actors onstage for my entertainment." She motioned to the kitchen doorway, which Prescott blocked. "Do give them my love."

"All right." He headed to the front door.

In her room, Tobias napped on the rug, and Maggie ruffled his ears. Then she turned on the little red Bakelite radio on her dresser so she wouldn't even be tempted to listen to the real-life drama in the living room.

After she pulled out her knitting, she settled into her armchair and tried to pay attention to *The Adventures of Superman*.

The next two hours dragged through news and serials and music. She made barely any progress on the left sleeve of the sweater for Rose, in her sister's favorite shade of yellow.

Twice she heard the bell.

Three times she unraveled rows she messed up.

Four times she stifled sobs. After everyone left, she'd indulge, but not yet.

A knock on her door. "Maggie?" Prescott said.

She turned off the radio and took a deep breath to smooth the ragged edges from her voice. "Yes? Do you need something?"

"I called the taxi company. Frank and Vi want to say goodbye."

She'd deliberately made herself frumpy so she wouldn't be lured into the limelight. "I didn't do this for me. It's a gift. An apology."

"They know that." His voice sounded softer and warmer than the wool in her hands. "They'd like to say goodbye."

"Not tonight."

Silence. No retreating footsteps. "Maggie? They're getting married."

Her mouth crumpled, and her eyes misted. "I—I'm so glad."

In the distance, the doorbell rang.

"The cab," Prescott said.

"Thank you for everything. And good night." But footsteps clomped down the hall. Had he heard her farewell?

After the front door opened and closed, Maggie left her bedroom.

The plates and silverware had already been cleared from the table. Yet another undeserved kindness from Prescott.

She blew out the candles, caught the whiff of Christmas-red roses.

In spite of Maggie, Frank and Vi would have their happy ending.

A strange sob billowed out, joy for her former friends mingled with grief for losing Prescott.

She picked up the salt and pepper shakers, but everything blurred around her.

Not yet. She needed to clean up, put away the food, wash the dishes.

The tears ignored her direction and made an unscripted entrance.

Prescott opened the cab door.

Vi hugged him. "Oh, Press, I'm so happy. Please tell Maggie."

"Tell her yourself tomorrow at the theater."

Frank shook his hand, grinning hard. "Thanks for everything. Best day of my life."

The young couple slid into the backseat, kissed, and waved at Prescott. The cab pulled away.

Now to help clean up.

The drapes were drawn in the bungalow, and Prescott pulled in a fortifying breath. He'd come resolved not to be moved by Maggie's beauty or cheer. He hadn't been prepared for the muting of both beauty and cheer. And the reason for the muting tore him up inside.

It was true remorse. Not only had she admitted she was wrong and worked to make things right, but she was actively fighting the impulses that had caused the problem in the first place. Fighting them too hard even.

Every detail tonight gleamed for Frank and Vi alone, even Maggie's removal of herself from the evening. She would accept no reward, not even the satisfaction of a job well done.

Prescott's resolve cracked in two.

What now? He pushed his feet up the walkway. Just because he loved her didn't mean they belonged together.

"Lord, help me listen." Maggie wasn't the only one who needed that lesson.

He opened the front door, and gulping sounds rose from the dining room.

At the table, Maggie sat with her face in her hands. She gasped and looked up, her face red and glistening. "You—I thought you left."

His feet froze. He could grab his hat and coat and make his escape. Except he hadn't called his own cab yet. "I'm helping clean up."

"No, no." She grabbed the saltshaker and darted past him and into the kitchen. "Didn't I mention? I told Ria. You don't need to clean up."

Prescott had the strangest sensation, as if he'd stepped into a place he didn't belong and a scene he wasn't meant to see, yet knowing—*knowing*—he was precisely where he belonged. In this place. In this scene. "I won't leave you with all these dishes."

"Nonsense." Her voice was high and trembling. "You've done enough."

One napkin lay damp and limp where Maggie had been seated. "You've been crying."

"I thought you left." Anger shuddered in her voice.

If those were happy tears for Frank and Vi, she would have said so. Prescott propelled himself deeper into this place of belonging and into the kitchen doorway. "What's wrong?"

Maggie ran water into the sink and shook in soap flakes—far more than needed. "You've already cleaned up my mess. You do not need to wash dishes. Good night."

Every scene had a tipping point, and Prescott stood firm. "What's wrong?"

Her shoulders hunched up in a brown dress that recalled the depths of the Depression. "Good night, Prescott. I vowed I wouldn't let you see me cry. I will not have you think I'm manipulating you with tears. Good night."

Prescott was the one tipping, falling, and he didn't want to stop. "Do you still love me?"

A cry of exasperation, and she scrubbed a plate so hard, water sloshed out of the sink. "No, I don't *still* love you. I love you more than ever. You could have let me suffer—should have—but no, you had to be nice to me. So yes, I'm crying. And now—wasn't it painful enough to be humbled? Why must I be humiliated as well? Would you please—please leave and let me keep one last shred of dignity?"

Prescott swayed as the day's events swirled around him like the dancers in "Winter Wonderland." The decisions he'd made, the contracts under negotiation, the dinner arranged to reunite lovers, to redress wrongs. All set in motion by this woman. This remarkable woman.

"Please listen to me." Her voice shattered into pieces. "I asked you to leave."

Instead, he listened to another voice in his head. "All my life, other people wrote my script, and I acted it out. Ma told me to leave, and I left. Men told me to work, and I worked. They told me to box, and I boxed."

Maggie ducked her head to the side and swiped her cheek on her shoulder.

Prescott stepped closer and braced himself against the oven, still warm from the dinner she'd prepared. "Melvin told me to act and sing and dance. And I stood where the director told me to stand, and I sang the lyrics they gave me, and I danced with whichever girl they put in my arms. Then I was burned, and they told me to stay out of sight, and I did."

A sniffle from Maggie. She adjusted the kerchief around her head, and an arc of droplets glittered in the air.

"These past few months—" His throat clogged.

"You wrote a new script." Her voice came out tiny. "I—I'm glad."

He had to be closer, and he leaned back against the sink beside her. "I met with Val Ruben today."

Her gaze bounced up to him. "You did?" Then she flinched and returned her attention to what had to be a very clean plate by now.

He'd never had a chance to tell her about the furious call from Melvin. "He wants to produce the script."

"Oh, Press." Her shiny cheeks quivered with a hint of a smile. "I'm so happy for you. I'm not surprised. It's a wonderful story. Oh, goodness. Your very own movie."

He held her with his gaze. "I owe it all to you."

"Nonsense." She sloshed around in the dishwater. "Your idea, your story, your words."

"Your encouragement." He set a hand on her forearm. "You're going to rub a hole clean through that plate."

A sobbing little chuckle, and she jerked her head to the side. She didn't move her arm.

With his scarred thumb, he caressed her arm in that damp brown sleeve. "The script for my new life is missing only one thing—my leading lady."

"No, Press." She wheeled to him. "Don't you dare. You know what I'm like, how I meddled, how—"

"How you humbled yourself, how—"

"No." Maggie wrenched her arm away and glared at him. "I won't let you do this. I want only the best for you, and I—"

"You are the best for me." He reached for her.

"I'm not. Please leave." She backed away, bumped into the icebox.

Prescott beckoned to her with his fingers, with a slight smile. "For a woman who claims to love me, you're trying awfully hard to talk me out of loving you. It won't work. I am madly in love with you. I'm not going anywhere."

She rubbed soapy hands on her belly, and her gaze darted in all directions. "Press . . ."

The distance was killing him, and he closed it and set his hands on her waist.

In the narrow space between them, her hands fluttered to her face. "Oh, Press. I look a fright."

"True."

Maggie gasped. "You aren't supposed to say that."

With a laugh, Prescott gathered her close. "No, I'm not. This is our big romantic scene. You're supposed to be in a glamorous evening gown with your hair and makeup just so. Like you were at the Del. How I wanted to kiss you that night."

A trembling smile, and she rested her forehead on his chest. "This isn't Hollywood."

"This is real life." He eased up her damp chin. "Sometimes

real-life heroines have red noses." He kissed that darling red nose. "And tear-stained cheeks." He tasted those sweet tears.

Reddened eyes glistened with love. "You haven't mentioned my pale lips."

"I was saving the best for last." And he savored those gorgeous pale lips.

SATURDAY, DECEMBER 25, 1943

The more time Prescott spent on Mr. Curtis's street in North Park, the more he liked it. The Craftsman bungalows, each different, stood far enough apart for privacy but close enough to know your neighbors.

This particular home drew him most. Prescott carried a bag of gifts up the walkway—small gifts, Maggie had insisted, since her family had just learned about him. Yesterday after the final performance at the Old Globe, he'd met Maggie's parents and sister.

He reached for the doorbell, but the door flew open. Maggie rushed out, shut the door, flung her arms about his neck, and gave him a luscious kiss.

"There," she said. "I can't do that in front of my family."

"Let's go, then." He backed toward the street.

She laughed and tugged his arm. "You can't get out of it that easily."

"Not that. I just want more kisses." The last ten days, they'd had only one day off from performances. Most of that day had been spent on business away from the woman he loved.

Maggie bestowed one more kiss and led him into the house,

filled with the smells of roasting turkey and a fire in the fireplace.

Mr. Curtis sat in his usual chair, and Prescott shook his hand before he could rise. An extra twinkle shone in the man's eyes now that his home was secure. After Prescott's private conversation last night with Mr. Curtis and Mr. Oliver, it was doubly secure.

Mr. Oliver shook Prescott's hand and studied him warily. "Merry Christmas."

"Merry Christmas, sir." It would take time for Prescott to build trust after that conversation, especially since he'd conducted it wearing a costume and greasepaint.

Mrs. Oliver gripped Prescott's hand in both of hers, with gentleness in her blue eyes. "We're glad you're here. Maggie can't stop talking about you."

Rose nodded, her own blue eyes wide. "Maggie loves you."

Maggie laughed and hugged her sister's shoulders. "Good thing I already told him."

"Maggie made this for me." Rose fiddled with her yellow sweater. "I like yellow."

"I do too," Prescott said. "Like the sun."

Rose's smile shone nearly as bright.

"Come, sit down." Maggie eased Prescott onto the sofa beside Rose, and Maggie perched on the sofa arm.

"I brought this for everyone to share, plus extra for you to take home." Prescott opened his bag and pulled out three boxes of Showley Brothers candy.

"Cluster Ruffs." Mrs. Oliver pressed fingers to her lips. "Oh, I've missed them."

Maggie kissed the top of Prescott's head. Apparently he'd done well. "Here's your gift." She set a slim box in his hand.

Inside lay a wide, ebony pen encased in a rubber grip. "Perfect for a writer," she said. "See how big it is? The stationer thinks adding the grip will help."

"It will." He hefted it and marveled at how it didn't slip from his fingers. "Thank you."

"I'll have it engraved with 'Joseph P. Duke.'" She settled another kiss on his head. "Where's my gift?"

"Maggie . . ." her mother said.

Maggie giggled and jiggled his shoulder. "Well?"

Prescott gave her an innocent smile and pointed to the candy. "Cluster Ruff?"

Her mouth fell open, rimmed in red lipstick he yearned to kiss away. "Prescott!"

He selected a piece of chocolate. "I'll give it to you at Frank and Vi's wedding."

"But that's two weeks away!"

"Twelve days. The twelfth day of Christmas."

A pout pushed out one pretty lip. "Won't you even tell me?"

"It's a secret." He took a bite of chocolate and nuts and maple cream. "You're right, Mrs. Oliver. These are good."

"A secret," Maggie said. "Isn't that ironic?"

"It is. But I know you'll like it. Optimistic of me. Arrogant even. But I did ask for advice."

"From . . . ?"

"From me, Maggie-mine," Mr. Curtis said with a pleased smile. "And from Ria."

"You know? Ria knows?" Maggie gaped at her grandfather and drummed her fingers on her crossed knees.

Mrs. Oliver stood. "Come, girls. Time to start the potatoes."

"But he's—"

"He's not telling." Prescott gave her his most serious look. "I see why you enjoy meddling. It's kind of fun."

"Oh my goodness." She planted a kiss on his cheek and followed her sister to the kitchen. "What have I done to you?"

What had she done indeed? She'd shown him the bright side, and now he intended to live in it.

THURSDAY, JANUARY 6, 1944

Sitting on the wooden pew in St. Francis Chapel in Balboa Park, Maggie kept her hand entwined with Prescott's.

In front of the carved altarpiece stood the bride and groom, Vi wearing a classy suit in pale green and Frank in his dress blues.

"You may kiss the bride," the naval chaplain said.

Frank leaned in, Vi met him, and they kissed.

Simply beautiful, and Maggie squeezed Prescott's hand, probably harder than she should have.

The organ in the balcony erupted in the recessional, and Petty Officer and Mrs. Sebastian proceeded down the aisle under the wood-beamed ceiling.

Vi caught Maggie's eye, and her smile grew.

Maggie smiled back and blinked hard. She still couldn't fathom Vi's forgiveness, Prescott's, the whole cast's. After Vi's dinner with Frank, the last wall of separation had collapsed. The shows had increased in polish and charm, even over the course of two weeks, performing to eighteen thousand servicemen and women.

The wedding guests, a mix of cast members and sailors, filed out of the little Spanish Colonial chapel, their shoes clicking on the red tile floor.

Prescott set his hand in the small of Maggie's back to guide her down the aisle. When they passed through the dark wood doors, he took her hand again and aimed an adoring smile down at her.

A thrill ran through her chest. Now for the reception in the lovely Alcazar Gardens, and the party made their way out to the Plaza de California, facing the grand façade of the California Tower.

Ria fell in beside them as they strolled through the plaza. "The perfect ending for a wonderful run of a show."

"It is." For the coming months, Maggie and Ria had booked Camp Shows troupes to perform at the Naval Air Station, the Naval Training Station, the Repair Base, Camp Pendleton, and other bases and camps in the area.

No directing, mostly coordinating, but the men would be well entertained.

Since Prescott would be busy in Hollywood, he wouldn't be performing.

After Christmas, he had returned to Beverly Hills, one hundred thirty miles from San Diego, and Maggie had seen him only twice. They'd had so little time to discuss how they'd continue to see each other.

She clutched Prescott's hand. Somehow they'd make it work. She loved him too much.

On the far side of the plaza, Ria turned right toward Alcazar Gardens.

But Prescott headed left across El Prado. "Bye, Ria. We'll see you later at the reception."

"Bye, you two."

"Where are we going?" Maggie asked.

"Time for your Christmas gift."

"Oh?" Her step perked up. Prescott wasn't carrying anything. Unless it was small enough to fit in his pocket.

Surely not . . .

Of course not. How arrogantly optimistic of her. Only a month had passed since their first kiss, a month that included a massive hiccup.

Prescott led her beside the California Tower, which stretched high to a cool blue sky speckled with clouds. "I've been busy this past week."

Maggie brushed against his arm. "I've missed you."

"I've missed you too." He gave her a soft look. "Which is why I had a long talk with Val and Melvin. You need to be here for your grandpa and your job, and I need to be with you."

Maggie slammed to a stop. "Your writing—you can't give it up."

"I've no intention of doing that." He resumed walking, passing the dome tiled in white and yellow and blue and green. "I wrote my first screenplay in my hotel room, at the beach, at your kitchen table. I can write anywhere. So I'll write in San Diego. I'll go to LA for meetings, occasionally for longer spells, but mostly here."

"That's wonderful. I'm thrilled." Then she frowned at him. "But your house."

"I'm renting it to the studio. They'll use it for new stars waiting to buy their own mansions. They'll leave the guesthouse for me to use." A satisfied smile creased the scars. "This past week I've been packing, preparing to have furniture shipped. To my new home."

Maggie stumbled over a crack in the pavement. "Your new . . . ?"

"That's my secret." He winked at her and led her into the plaza in front of the Old Globe Theatre. "Your grandpa calls it the

Fortner place, across the street from his place, one block up. Two-story Craftsman, wood shingle siding."

"I know the house." Maggie stared at him. "I've always liked it."

"Now it's the Duke place. I bought it the Wednesday before Christmas. Your grandpa came with me, made sure it was sound, told me what repairs are needed. Ria came too. I—I wanted a woman's opinion."

A laugh flowed out. "You'll be so close. That's the best gift I could imagine."

"That's not the gift. You see, this whole meddling scheme of mine hinges on you. And I did meddle." Furrows formed across his brow.

"What do you mean?" She'd never seen him look so guilty.

"Remember when I met your parents after the final show on Christmas Eve? When I took your father and grandfather outside for a chat?"

"Yes." Whatever had he done? Maggie stopped in front of the circular theater with its half-timbering near the roof.

He faced her and stared down at their clasped hands. "I told your father that your grandpa needs to remain in his house, and that if your wages don't meet his needs, I'll cover any gaps. I discussed this with your grandpa beforehand, the day I bought the house."

How incredibly kind of him—and how courageous. "Papa—I doubt he liked that."

A chuckle, and he played with Maggie's fingers. "Not one bit. A complete stranger—an actor wearing greasepaint, nonetheless—meddling in his family. But once I explained my Christmas gift for you . . ." His voice rasped.

What did her gift have to do with Grandpa?

Prescott released her hand and fished in his pocket. "It would be different if I were helping family." He held out a jewelry box of midnight blue velvet.

Maggie's hands flew to her mouth.

With his face agitating, Prescott glanced over his shoulder at the Old Globe. "In *Twelfth Night*, two couples have happy endings—one couple married, the other on their way. Now Frank and Vi are married, and you and I . . ."

He snapped open the box. A square-cut diamond rested in a platinum setting, bordered by an Art Deco band of tiny diamonds—were there twelve of them?—yes, twelve.

Maggie's fingers trembled on her lips. It was so lovely, so perfect.

"I know it's early." Prescott's voice grated, and he dragged his gaze up to her, liquid and warm. "I also know I love you and want you beside me for the rest of my life. If you're not ready, I'll hold on to this, try again later. But I'm not giving up, Maggie Oliver."

Words twirled in her head, and not one could pass her lips.

"I'll be right across the street." He tipped his head. "If you agree to marry me, we'll be right across the street from your grandpa. We can cook for him, help him, enjoy his company, take him to the movies and the zoo. He'll be in his home, filled with memories of his beloved. And I hope to fill my new home with memories of my beloved."

Maggie's eyes filled. She didn't deserve his love or a future with him, but she'd be foolish to turn down such a gift. With a shuddering breath, she lowered her hands from her mouth. "As Olivia says in *Twelfth Night*, 'Love sought is good, but given unsought, is better.'"

Brown eyes darkened with wistful longing. "Does that mean . . . ?"

She raised her quivering left hand.

A smile hopped around on his lips, and he plucked at the ring. "I may need help. Not terribly romantic of me to drop it."

Maggie slipped the ring onto her finger, a bit snug, but she didn't care. "Oh, Press. I love it. I love you. Do you think the chaplain is still in the chapel? He could marry us right now."

A big laugh rolled from his gorgeous mouth, and he took her by the waist and pulled her close. "I promised your father a long engagement."

She wound her arms around his neck and kissed him. "How long? One week? Two? Please not twelve. Not everything has to be in twelves."

He kissed her back, far too short. "We were negotiating in months, not weeks."

Maggie caressed the back of his neck. "Are you done meddling?"

"You may now enter the negotiations." He nuzzled a kiss onto her forehead. "As I told you on the phone the day you invited me into your USO show, 'I'm yours, Miss Oliver.'"

He was. She stood surrounded by the rustle of palm trees and the scent of eucalyptus and the joy of Prescott's love. "And I am yours."

AUTHOR'S NOTE

Dear Reader,

I hope you enjoyed the show with Prescott and Maggie!

After the United States implemented a peacetime draft in September 1940, training camps sprang up around the nation, and the influx of troops overwhelmed small towns. Civilian organizations helped meet the needs of the troops. On February 4, 1941, the six main groups—the Young Men's Christian Association, Young Women's Christian Association, National Jewish Welfare Board, National Catholic Community Service, Traveler's Aid Association, and Salvation Army—came together to found the United Service Organizations (USO).

Entirely civilian run and civilian funded, the USO established over three thousand clubs in the US and overseas, sent mobile units to remote training sites, set up lounges and canteens at bus and railroad terminals, and far more.

To entertain troops at home and abroad, USO-Camp Shows was established on October 30, 1941. Over seven thousand men and women performed for the USO in World War II, with big stars donating their time for free. By May 1945, Camp Shows produced over seven hundred shows daily.

The San Diego Army-Navy YMCA was built in 1924 and was run by the USO during World War II. At its peak, it served eight million guests in 1944—twenty-one thousand each day! The tile floor in the lobby really did wear out in only one year.

Balboa Park is a treasure. Not only a gorgeous urban park, it features structures from the 1915–1916 Panama-California Exposition and the 1935 California Pacific Exposition, now home to excellent museums. To expand the naval hospital, the US Navy requisitioned many of the buildings on December 10, 1941 (including the Old Globe), and more on March 5, 1943. The San Diego Zoo, founded in 1921, remained open during the war—and the stories of the baby hippo and Trudy the Tapir are true!

After the 1935 Exposition, the Old Globe Theatre was to be torn down, but the city raised money, and a rebuilt structure opened on December 2, 1937. During the war, the Navy used it for lectures and entertainment, and Bob Hope performed there with the USO. Sadly, the theater was destroyed by fire in 1978. In 1982, a new theater opened and is active today. The new theater isn't exactly like the original, but it's beautiful.

Thank you for visiting World War II San Diego with me.

ACKNOWLEDGMENTS

My name may be on the "marquee," but this novella had a huge cast and crew bring it to stage.

The story wouldn't exist if it weren't for my dear friend—and talented author!—Karen Barnett. Several years ago, Karen invited me to contribute a Christmas novella to a collection centered on vintage theaters.

The thought of a Christmas USO show in San Diego flitted into my head, and then I read about the Old Globe Theatre in Balboa Park and the one-hour Shakespeare plays, including *Twelfth Night*, performed for the 1935 California Pacific Exposition. From there, my story idea flew together. We were unable to find a home for our collection of novellas, but Prescott and Maggie wouldn't leave me alone. I'm so glad I had the chance to write their story.

As always, I'm thankful for my critique partners, Sherry Kyle and Judy Gann. Since Judy was raised in San Diego, she was extraordinarily helpful with local information, and she showed me to some amazing websites.

Many thanks to the docents who conduct the fascinating behind-the-scenes tours of the Old Globe Theatre. Since our tour group was very small, our docent—once he heard about my project—showed us old photographs of the theater, which were amazing to see.

My incredible cast and crew include my family and my friends from church and our neighborhood and the writing world. My "producers and directors" include my agent, Rachel Kent, my editors, Rachel McRae and Kristin Kornoelje, and Karen Steele and Rachael Betz in publicity and marketing.

As a former Navy mom, I'm thankful for the work of the USO, which continues its mission to provide a "home away from home" for men and women serving in the military.

Just as a show only comes to life in the presence of an audience, a book comes to life in the presence of readers. I write for you and because of you, and I'm thankful for each one of you. Please visit me at www.SarahSundin.com to leave a message, sign up for my email newsletter, read about the history behind the story, and see photos of Balboa Park and San Diego.

DISCUSSION QUESTIONS

1. At the beginning of the story, Maggie receives a difficult assignment on short notice. How does she make do? How do others help her? Have you ever found yourself in a similar tight spot? How did you handle it?

2. "Prescott knew dashed dreams, knew how the shards of them carved you up inside." How do you see this—not just in Prescott's life, but in the lives of other characters? How do each of them overcome the loss of dreams? How have you dealt with lost dreams?

3. Maggie's determination to find—or make—a bright side inspires Prescott, as does her advice for him to write a new script for his life. How does her encouragement cause him to grow? Have you had an encourager like Maggie in your life?

4. Prescott's visit to the naval hospital propels him to change his life. How did you see this? What can you

glean from his revelation? Have unexpected events ever changed the course of your life?

5. Despite her protests to the contrary, Maggie meddles. Where does this desire come from? How does it help—and hurt people? How does she change? What do you think of Grandpa's advice, "If you're keeping secrets, you're meddling"?

6. Bill Curtis is a key character in this story, driving Maggie's work and drawing Prescott into a place of belonging. What did you think of these relationships?

7. Maggie is reluctant to alter her dreams, from streamlining her show to reuniting Vi and Frank. Prescott is too quick to give up his dreams, from screenwriting to pursuing Maggie. How do they teach each other? Which character are you more like?

8. Grandpa tells Maggie that prayer is more than listing—it's listening. How does this play out in the story? Do you have problems with the listening part of prayer?

9. Prescott struggles with idleness. How does he overcome it? How does he find purpose? Have you seen the dangers of idleness or the joy of purpose in your own life?

10. Maggie sees a kernel of arrogance in optimism, and Prescott sees a kernel of self-pity in pessimism. What are the strengths and weaknesses of each mindset? How can each benefit from the other?

11. Have you ever performed onstage—whether singing, acting, or dancing? What did you enjoy about it? Did this story remind you of those moments?

12. Just for fun! In each chapter, I've scattered "Easter eggs"—more appropriately "Christmas eggs"—related to the corresponding days in "The Twelve Days of Christmas." Did you notice any? How many did you find?

Sarah Sundin is the bestselling and Christy Award–winning author of eighteen World War II novels, including *Mists over the Channel Islands*, *Midnight on the Scottish Shore*, and *Embers in the London Sky*. Her novel *Until Leaves Fall in Paris* won the 2022 Christy Award, *The Sky Above Us* received the 2020 Carol Award, and *The Sound of Light*, *When Twilight Breaks*, and *The Land Beneath Us* were finalists for the Christy Award.

During WWII, one of her grandfathers served as a pharmacist's mate (medic) in the US Navy, and her great-uncle flew with the US Eighth Air Force. Her other grandfather, a professor of German, helped train American soldiers in the German language through the US Army Specialized Training Program.

Sarah and her husband live in Southern California and have three adult children and two adorable grandchildren. Their two rescue dogs make sure she gets plenty of walks and fresh air. Sarah enjoys teaching Sunday school and speaking for church, community, and writers' groups. She also serves as co-director of the West Coast Christian Writers Conference. Visit www.SarahSundin.com for more information.

GET TO KNOW

SARAH SUNDIN

To Learn More about Sarah,

Read Her Blog, or See

the Inspiration behind the Stories,

Visit

SARAHSUNDIN.COM